Praise for Thomas Greanias

'Combines good old-fashioned suspense with throat-grabbing twists. Just the right blend of science, myth, history and action. Marvellous!' STEVE BERRY

'Lightning-paced, dagger-sharp and brilliantly executed' JAMES ROLLINS

'A giddily-paced, rollicking, globe-spanning tale of adventure, discovery and derring-do that pulled me in from the first page. It's rare to find a tale as well researched as it is entertaining' CHRISTOPHER REICH

'A rollercoaster that will captivate readers of Dan Brown and Michael Crichton, penetrating the biggest mystery of our time' *Washington Post*

'Thomas Greanias combines the pace of Dan Brown with the persuasion of Michael Crichton. A definite winner' *Chicago Tribune*

A former journalist, media executive and screenwriter, Thomas Greanias is the founder and CEO of Atlantis Interactive Inc., a Beverly Hills-based entertainment company that has created some of the Web's most groundbreaking entertainment.

Visit www.thomasgreanias.com

Also by Thomas Greanias

The Atlantis Revelation
The Atlantis Prophecy
Raising Atlantis

THE
PROMISED
WAR

Thomas Greanias

POCKET
BOOKS

LONDON • SYDNEY • NEW YORK • TORONTO

First published in the USA by Atria Books, 2010
A division of Simon & Schuster Inc.
First published in Great Britain by Simon & Schuster UK Ltd, 2010
This edition first published by Pocket Books, 2010
An imprint of Simon & Schuster UK Ltd
A CBS COMPANY

1 3 5 7 9 10 8 6 4 2

Simon & Schuster UK Ltd
1st Floor
222 Gray's Inn Road
London
WC1X 8HB

www.simonandschuster.co.uk

Simon & Schuster Australia
Sydney

A CIP catalogue record for this book
is available from the British Library

B Format ISBN 978-1-84983-035-5

Printed in the UK by CPI Cox & Wyman, Reading, Berkshire RG1 8EX

*To friends Mark and Melinda, Bill and Priscilla,
Frank and Jeanne, Skip and Lara and all who have
devoted their lives to breaking down the world's walls of
misunderstanding through their love and compassion
to people of every race, color and creed.*

They did not gain possession of the land by their own sword,
but by your mighty hand, because you favored them.

—Zabur 44:3 (Psalm 44:3)

THE PROMISED LAND

**LAND OF CANAAN
1400 B.C.**

ARAMEANS

Mount Lebanon

Tyre

SIDONIANS

Mount Hermon • Damascus

HIVITES

• Hazor
• Merom

Lake Huldah

HITTITES

• Chinnereth

BASHAN

Sea of Chinnereth

Mount Carmel

GIRGASHITES

Mount Tabor

Dor

Mount Gilboa

GREAT SEA

Plain of Sharon

CANAANITES

• Tirzah

PERIZZITES

• Shechem

• Shiloh

• Adam

Jordan River

HIVITES

AMORITES

Aijalon •
• Bethel
• Gibeon
• Ai

Gilgal ⊙

Valley of Shittim

• Makkedah
• Gibeah

AMMONITES

• Lachish
Eglon •

⊙ Jericho

Gaza •

PHILISTINES

JEBUSITES

Debir •

Mount Nebo

• Beersheba

Salt Sea (Dead Sea)

MOABITES

• Hornah

AMORITES

LAND OF CANAAN

Kadesh-Barnea •

HITTITES

EDOMITES

• Zoar

MIDIANITES

1

The Dome of the Rock mosque rose like the moon behind the towering wall that surrounded the Temple Mount. Sam Deker cleared the top of the wall and dropped into the gardens below, a wraith in the night. He glanced at the illuminated hands of his Krav Maga watch. Seven minutes to three. He had told Stern fourteen minutes back at the van. He had used up six. Time was running out.

Deker reached into his combat pack and pulled out a brick of C-4. He had enough bricks to take out half of the thirty-five-acre complex. If he had any doubts about this operation, now was the moment to turn back. He slipped the C-4 back into his pack and moved through the maze of trees and shrubs.

The Temple Mount was the most contested religious site in the world. For Muslims, the eight-sided, golden-capped Dome of the Rock mosque protected the "noble rock" that they believed to be the foundation stone of the earth and the place from which the prophet Muhammad ascended to heaven.

But religious Jews believed the rock was the place from which God gathered the dust to create the first man, Adam, as well as the site of King Solomon's Temple. According to Jewish prophecy, it was also where a new temple would be built—once the Dome of the Rock was gone. Many of these Jews, like Deker's fanatical superior officer, Colonel Uri Elezar, refused to set foot on such holy ground.

None of this was a problem for Deker. He could care less. Deker had been recruited by Israel's internal security service, the Shin Bet, precisely because he was a secular American Jew who had served with the U.S. Marines in Iraq and Afghanistan as a demolitions officer. Who better to protect the Temple Mount, he was told, than a twenty-six-year-old who specialized in the destruction of major structures and equally offended both sides of the religious divide?

Deker followed the route he had planned well in advance, timing his steps with the movements of the Palestinian security guards of the Islamic Waqf, or religious trust.

For almost a thousand years the Waqf had served as the protectors of the Temple Mount, even after Israel captured Jerusalem in the 1967 Arab-Israeli War. Such was their status as the true guardians of Islam—and allegedly above the petty political interests of the modern Palestinian Authority, which claimed it had sovereignty over the site.

Deker, however, knew the Waqf to be as political as any Muslim organization; it simply saw the Arab-Israeli struggle in terms of centuries, not decades. So far as the Waqf was concerned, Israel's resurrection as a modern state in 1948 after three thousand years of exile was but a foul blot on the long scroll of history.

Israel, meanwhile, decided it best to prevent unnecessary provocations by its own more zealous citizens. So not only did it allow the Waqf to continue to manage the Temple Mount, it even enforced a controversial ban on Jewish prayers there.

When Deker finally reached the east wall of the Dome of the Rock mosque, he pressed his back against the blue ceramic tiles of the outer wall and peered around the corner. A Waqf guard was making his way across the vast plaza toward the other mosque on the Mount, the silver-capped Al-Aqsa. Deker waited until the guard passed under the *ma'avzin* arches and disappeared down the steps to the lower plaza. Then without hesitation he darted across the colonnaded entrance of the mosque and ducked inside.

The Waqf officer in charge that night was rounding one of the titanic marble columns that supported the dome twenty meters overhead when Deker entered the mosque. The Palestinian managed to grab his radio, but before he could engage the device to transmit even a sound, Deker gave him a chop to the throat. He crumpled to the floor.

Deker made sure the guard still had a pulse before he turned to his right and followed the plush ruby carpet to the steps that led down to a cave dedicated to King Solomon. A relic of the Crusades, the cave had been carved out by the Order of Knights Templar after they had converted the Dome of the Rock into their Templum Domini, or "Temple of Our Lord."

Medieval maps marked the cave as the "center of the world," and the "well of souls" beneath it was said to have once served as the resting place of the legendary lost Ark of the Covenant. According to the ancient biblical account, the sacred Ark—an ornate box made of shittimwood and coated with gold—contained the original Ten Commandments, the tablets that God gave to Moses at Mount Sinai as the ancient Israelites wandered the desert in search of the Promised Land. Deker thought God—Yahweh to the Israelites—should have simply given Moses a map. It would have saved the Israelites forty years and countless lives.

But the Knights Templar couldn't hold the Temple Mount for long. A few years later it was back in the hands of the Muslim Waqf, where it had remained that past millennium.

Recently, the Waqf had quietly begun a massive subterranean tunneling operation. The Israel Defense Forces, or IDF, feared that the Waqf was on the verge of discovering an ancient network of chambers and corridors deep beneath the mount that predated even the First and Second Jewish Temples. The front door to that network was none other than the well of souls beneath the Dome of the Rock.

Adjan Husseini, the Palestinian head of the Waqf in Jerusalem, was kneeling facedown in prayer when Deker entered the cave. At the sound of Deker's footsteps, he lifted his head and started at the sight of the C-4 brick Deker removed from his pack.

Looking Husseini in the eye, Deker held the brick up and said, "Boom."

"Commander Deker." Husseini rose to his feet. "Go ahead. Take the shot."

Deker put the C-4 brick back into his pack and took out his BlackBerry. Draping one arm around Husseini's neck, he extended the other and snapped a photo with his phone's camera. He then e-mailed it to Colonel Elezar.

"It's time-stamped," Deker said, putting the phone away. "I copied you too."

But Husseini, eyes wide, was staring at the explosives and blinking LED displays inside Deker's open pack, catching on that the C-4 charges were real. "You could have blown us all to bits!"

Deker said, "I promised you that I would expose loopholes in your security in the hopes you'd finally relent and let us put up the electronic surveillance net."

"So you can spy on us."

"So we can better defend the Dome of the Rock from the ultra-Orthodox Jews who want to destroy it so that they can erect a Third Temple. Or from radical Palestinians who would pin the blame on Orthodox Jews. You've seen the intel. The threat's real and it's imminent."

Husseini said nothing for a moment. A hole in the six-foot rock ceiling allowed a shaft of light from the mosque above to illuminate several small altars and prayer niches around the chamber. Deker could see Husseini's eyes study him with bitter resentment through the haze of incense and flickering candlelight.

"You knew from the start that we'd never agree to Israeli surveillance," Husseini said. "Yet, you proceeded to pull this dangerous stunt only to humiliate us."

Husseini was baiting him now, stalling. Deker sensed a trap and realized he had no idea where the Waqf guards outside were at the moment. He thought of Stern back at the van. It was time to leave.

"This security test isn't nearly as dangerous as the weapons cache you've been stockpiling in the southeast corner under Solomon's Stables," Deker said.

Surprise registered on Husseini's face, although Deker wasn't sure if it was real or manufactured by the man.

"Oh, yes, we know about that," Deker told him. "And that tunnel you've been digging right under this cave. If anyone is going to start the fire, it's going to be you."

Husseini picked up a bronze candelabra and brought it down heavily onto the floor's marble slab. It gave out a hollow thud, revealing the existence of a lower chamber, the well of souls. His face was an unreadable mask again.

"Is that really your concern here tonight, Commander Deker? Or are you afraid we might find something that Israel has been hiding from the world? Wise men have long believed that a cosmic portal exists here, a tunnel through space and time that leads to paradise."

Deker paused. "Or maybe it's the gate to hell."

Husseini was angry now. The expression on his face didn't show it, and his voice was steady and subdued. But his words were bitter and sharp.

"You think you're so special, Deker—better than the rest of us. That you're the human pin in a live grenade, standing alone between old Arabs like me and Jews like your Colonel Elezar. But know this: the Jews won't stop until they have destroyed the dome above us. Armageddon is inevitable. It's a time bomb that will go off. You can't stop it. Just like you couldn't prevent your girlfriend from blowing herself up with an explosive made by your own hands."

Deker felt the world give way under his feet at the thought of his Rachel and the horrible mistake he had made that had cost her her life. But he stood firm, emotionless in his expression, and turned to face Husseini, who picked up a ceremonial washbowl with a candle from the altar.

"I'm told the device looked something like this," Husseini said, stroking the red and black ceramic pattern. "You and your IDF masters intended to assassinate a Hamas militant inside the home of a Palestinian government official. But by some mystery known only to Allah, you mixed up the bowls, and the one with the explosive ended up in the hands of your beloved as she prepared to light her Shabbat candles to celebrate the first night of the Passover at the Western Wall. Mercifully, she perished the instant you hit your remote detonator. News reports said the six injured Jews around her took several hours to die."

In that second, Deker wanted to reach over and rip out Husseini's throat. And he would have, if he didn't know that's exactly what Husseini wanted him to attempt.

"The grief of your error must torment you every waking hour and haunt you in your sleep," Husseini went on, the corners of his mouth turning into a slight smile at having gotten even the suppression of a reaction out of him. "Perhaps that's why you can't leave this place. To you it was always a holy pile of rubbish, but to her it was her faith and life. Now it's her tombstone and you are a ghost stumbling in the graveyard of history. But it's impossible to bring her back. We can't change the past any more than we can change the future."

"That hasn't stopped you from trying." Deker produced a pottery shard he had found in an open trench at the base of the eastern wall. He pointed it like a dagger at Husseini's chest. "Your bulldozers are destroying ancient First and Second Temple artifacts. As if you can erase Israel from history."

Husseini's eyes flickered in fear for the first time that night as he looked at the shard in Deker's hand, clenched so tight that Deker didn't know he had cut himself until he felt a trickle of blood through his fingers. The Palestinian seemed to realize he had pushed Deker too far, but he stood defiant.

"Keeping your dead lover's memory alive doesn't change the fact that Jerusalem has always been an Arab and Islamic city," Husseini said, sticking with the party line to the end. "This piece of pottery you are waving at me is a plant. No Jewish temple ever stood here."

"Right," Deker said, placing the bloodstained shard on the small altar as a souvenir of this encounter. "Neither did I."

"Would that were true," Husseini told him. "But a man at war with himself can't keep the peace forever. You have a gift for destruction. You cannot suppress the expression of your nature forever. You will set the fire, not us. Because you *are* the fire. A tool to be used by your masters."

Deker wiped his bloodied hand on his trouser leg, gave him a slight bow and turned toward the cave entrance. He then vanished up the steps, leaving Husseini to his prayers.

. . .

Three minutes later—and six minutes later than he had promised Stern—Deker rappelled over the eastern wall and landed on the roof of a yellow Caterpillar backhoe loader parked against the base. He jumped off and raced down the slope of the Muslim graveyard abutting the wall, weaving his way through the tombstones toward the parked Gihon Water and Sewage Company service van.

He stopped the second he saw the cracked windshield and unmistakable bullet hole.

Deker whipped out his Jericho 9mm pistol from his pack and rushed to the driver's side of the van, aiming his Jericho through the window with one hand as he threw open the door with the other. Stern was slumped over the wheel, motionless. Deker felt sick with rage. He pushed Stern's head with the steel nose of his gun. The head rolled to the side, lifeless, revealing a bloody hole in the temple.

A flash in the driver's-side mirror caught Deker's eye and he glanced back to see a black van barreling up from behind. In the same motion, Deker jumped into the Gihon van, pushed Stern's corpse away and slid behind the wheel. He heard the squeal of brakes and the crash of boots on the ground. As he turned the ignition and shifted gears, the glass behind him shattered.

He felt a prick in the back of his neck and he lurched forward into the dashboard. His head hanging down, everything spinning, he saw Stern's twisted face staring at him before everything exploded in a burst of light.

2

The flash of light faded and Deker woke up to a nightmare of pain and confusion. His head was being knocked to and fro by the butt of a gun. He blinked his eyes open to see his superior officer, Uri Elezar, handcuffed and hanging upside down on a Nazi-style "Boger swing" with a rod behind his knees, his mouth open in agony. But Deker couldn't hear anything. Then another whack to the head opened his ears, and something like the whine of a jet engine filled his head before it faded into an irritating ring and Elezar's screams filled the room.

"We are the Jewish people!" Elezar shouted. "We came to this land by a miracle! God brought us back to this land! We fight to expel the non-Jews who are interfering with our conquest of this holy land!"

Deker watched a large figure standing next to Elezar strike the soles of his blackened feet and his back with a truncheon. Elezar cried out, and Deker saw drops of blood from Elezar's cut forehead hit the tile floor. The floor was covered with white powder, possibly salt, and underneath Deker could see a Byzantine mosaic.

"We are the Jewish people!" Elezar again rasped loudly. "We came to this land by a miracle! God brought us back to this land! We fight to expel the non-Jews who are interfering with our conquest of this holy land!"

A large face with dark hooded eyes appeared in front of Deker, and a hand reached out and snatched the silver Star of David hanging around Deker's neck and dangled it before his eyes. The IDF insignia in the center came in and out of focus. Then a hand snapped his head back, thick fingers pulled his eyelids apart and a hot beam of light blinded him.

A voice in English with a thick Arab accent said, "Still with us, Jew? Maybe we'll have better luck with you."

The accent of his torturer, the *farruj*-style beating of Elezar and the mosaic on the floor suggested to Deker that the enemy in the room was the General Intelligence Department, or GID, the Hashemite Kingdom of Jordan's powerful spy and security agency. All of which didn't make any sense, as Jordan was at peace with Israel and a proven ally of the United States in the war on terror. But it told him was that he wasn't getting out alive.

It's over. Now the game is to go out without compromising Israel.

Deker blinked his swollen eyes open again and saw that he was inside a dark stone chamber—a basement of some kind. A second man with long black hair stood over a small bank of medical equipment.

"Before the sun rises in a couple of hours, a large portion of the Temple Mount will collapse, and it will look like you two here did it on behalf of the Orthodox Jewish fanatics," the Jordanian said. "Palestinian rioters will overrun Jerusalem, raise the Palestinian flag, and Israel won't be able to stop the world from recognizing the capital of the new nation of Palestine."

"That could work," Deker said. "But it won't. Or else you would have already killed me and Elezar."

Like Stern, Deker thought, heaping more guilt upon himself. He remembered how his driver had been jumpy about the mission from the start—for good reason, as it turned out. Then his thoughts turned to Stern's young wife, Jenny, and their eighteen-month-old son, David. He had failed to protect them, like he had failed to protect Rachel. But he would not fail Israel now, he vowed to himself. He could not. It was all he had left to live for and to die for.

"The Tehown," the Jordanian said, using the Hebrew code name for Israel's top-secret fail-safe. "Tell me about this so-called gate of the deep or tunnel of chaos that will save the Jews but kill the Arabs. We need to know what kind of Jewish physics we're dealing with."

Deker now understood what this was about. He was one of only three Israelis besides the prime minister who knew the secret of the Tehown. Not even his superiors in the IDF knew its details, including Elezar, for fear they would use it before its intended time as Israel's last resort.

Elezar began to shout, "I'll kill you myself if you break, Deker! I swear it! I'll kill you myself!"

The Jordanian nodded to the guard next to Elezar, who shoved an electric prod into the IDF veteran's groin and delivered enough blue voltage to knock him out and create a thin wisp of smoke.

"Your superior officer is rather annoying, don't you think?" the Jordanian asked. "He is certainly no friend of yours. Look what he sent out earlier this evening."

The Jordanian held up Deker's BlackBerry so that Deker could read a Twitter alert from the Jerusalem Highway Patrol, complete with his picture.

Deker looked at himself on the small screen. The stone-faced expression made Deker himself wonder if a heart could still be beating inside this man. Only the dark, half-dead eyes revealed the faintest smolder of a passion snuffed out by life a long time ago.

> 12:43 a.m. Male. 26. 5'11". Brown hair. Gray
> eyes. Armed and extremely dangerous. Shoot if
> subject resists arrest.

"That last order seemed completely uncalled-for," the Jordanian said in a flat voice, thick with sarcasm. "And these are supposed to be your people."

That Elezar and the Shin Bet never wanted him to succeed in persuading the Waqf to acquiesce to an electronic surveillance net didn't surprise him. If anything, after a botched assassination attempt in Dubai a couple of years back that caught Mossad agents on camera, his superiors preferred to avoid a repeat the next time they had to storm the Temple Mount and kill a few Waqf guards.

Nor was he surprised that the Jordanian attempting to break him now would use Elezar's APB to divide his Israeli captives.

But Deker was indeed surprised by the shoot-to-kill order.

I'll deal with Elezar and the IDF once I escape, he vowed to himself. But first he would have to escape. To do that, he'd have to kill their captors and see just where on earth they had been taken. If they were in the basement of the GID HQ in Amman, he and Elezar were finished. But Deker didn't think so. They were probably still close to Jerusalem, perhaps in some safe house in Jericho or the West Bank.

If so, we still have a chance.

Without warning, the Jordanian struck him on the side of the head. A flash of light exploded before his eyes.

"The Tehown fail-safe, Commander!" he yelled with a maniacal growl. "What is the nature of the fail-safe?"

As the howls echoed in his ears, and the flash of light dissipated, Deker could see a glowing cord extend out from a bank of computer screens. It traveled straight toward his head, just above his eye, where it seemed to bore into his skull.

What the hell? This experiment had gone beyond anything in the GID playbook—or anything else he had ever experienced.

Pure panic now overwhelmed him as he realized with horror that there was a shunt in his head with a thin intravenous line attached, some sort of fiber-optic cable pulsating with a neon purple light.

Deker winced as the Jordanian pressed on a button and suddenly another blast of lightning flashed before Deker's burning eyes. The unbearable pain lingered like a mushroom cloud inside Deker's head. When the overexposure finally lifted, he could see the ghost of its outlines.

Deker struggled to catch his breath. Terror tore his conscience as he sensed whatever human resolve was left in him was beginning to wither. "I'll tell you how to wipe the Zionist state off the map," he said desperately, gasping. "But you won't like it and you won't do it, because you all have your heads up your asses."

"I'm listening," said the Jordanian, for once without the threat of imminent violence in his voice.

"Call their bluff," Deker told him, aware of Elezar beginning to stir in his chains. "Lay down your arms. Ask to be fully recognized citizens of Israel. Israel is already ten percent Arab, the West Bank almost ten percent Jewish. Two states side by side is apartheid. Nothing changes. One state with an Arab majority risks Israel losing its Jewish identity."

"Never!" Elezar shouted, fully awake now and aware of Deker's words. "I'd sooner have two states and keep the foreign dogs in their pounds."

"See," Deker said with a weak smile. "Our heads are up our asses too. So tell me, Hamas or Hezbollah or whoever you are. What do you want? More rockets? I can get them for you. More explosives? Just tell me how you want them delivered. The more you lob rockets, the more you secure the borders of a greater Israel and hurt your own. You are Israel's secret fail-safe."

The Jordanian was not amused. He was about to fire another burst of light when Deker's hand reached out for the rod behind Elezar's knees. In one smooth motion he slid it out from the chains with a yank and struck the Jordanian on the back of his head with all the force he could muster. As his captor, still conscious but dazed, put his hands up to his head, Deker reached down and pulled out the Jordanian's sidearm and turned as the other one fired a shot. Deker used the stunned Jordanian as a shield for the oncoming bullet and returned fire, killing his captor with a bullet between the eyes.

Deker looked up to see Elezar, dangling in his chains with the rod removed.

"Get me out!" shouted Elezar, unimpressed by Deker's latest feat.

Deker unchained Elezar. His superior officer fell to the floor and gasped as his bloody bare soles touched the ground as he rose to his feet.

"Thank you very much, Commander," Elezar said tightly, and punched Deker in the face, sending another flash of light across Deker's skull. "You think this erases what you've done? I warned the PM not to sign off on your crazy scheme to test the Waqf at the Temple Mount. You thought you were testing their defenses. It's clear now that they were testing you—the IDF's weakest link."

Deker had to steady himself for a moment. Elezar's weakened fist didn't land all that hard a blow. But Deker felt as if there were some kind of splinter in his brain and found the sensation unnerving. "Your text alert calling me dangerous didn't help."

"I had to stop you before it was too late," Elezar said. "Instead I find Stern dead at the wheel, and myself captured and tortured."

Stern, thought Deker as another wave of guilt washed over him again.

"Who knows what you've told them?" Elezar went on. "Even you don't seem to know. Our business isn't over, Deker. You will answer for this failure in security."

"What failure in security, Elezar? You getting captured?"

"No, fool. You're the lowest in the chain of command with knowledge of the fail-safe. They're going to use whatever you told them along with your breach of the Temple Mount tonight as a pretext for their own attack and pin the blame on us."

It was bad, Deker knew, worse than he could comprehend at the moment. Still, they had to keep moving, and that meant ignoring the hot-blooded Elezar's commentary second-guessing everything he did. He had grown used to it over the years. "Let's go," he said, grabbing his BlackBerry and explosives pack.

They moved quickly down the outside corridor, the hum of the air-conditioning heavy in the air, and slowed down at intersections with other hallways. But they encountered nobody else and reached a metal door. Deker slid the heavy metal bolt aside and paused. He eased the door open, heart beating as it scraped too loudly against the stone step, and they stepped out into the night.

The horizon was a moonscape dotted with squat, whitewashed concrete boxes, rooftop satellite dishes and minarets. But there was also the unmistakable silhouette of an old Byzantine church on a hill.

Deker's heart sank. They were much farther from freedom than he had hoped.

"We're in Madaba," he told Elezar. "'City of Mosaics.'"

"Jordan? How do you know?"

"The mosaic on the floor inside—they're in half the old houses here. And St. George's Greek Orthodox Church over there. It has that famous tiled mosaic map of Palestine on the floor. Most Christian town in Jordan. Very tolerant."

"For Christians and Muslims," said Elezar, "not for Jews like us. Not if bad elements of the GID are involved."

"If we're lucky, we can reach the border in twenty-five minutes," Deker said, working his BlackBerry. "But I can't get a signal on my phone, and the GID is going to know we've escaped in five, if they don't already."

Deker checked his pack for his Jericho 9mm, but it was missing. The memory of his last moments struggling in the service van flitted across his brain, and he realized his gun was probably back in that van. His zipped his pack closed with a yank of frustration, then set off down the stone steps toward the street, Elezar behind him.

Deker crept close to the wall, slowing at the end of the alley to motion Elezar to pause while he peered into the street. He felt naked without his gun, vulnerable and angry. And his head pounded. His eyes should have adjusted to the dark by now, but his vision seemed dull and blurry. When a car came down the street, Deker pushed his back against the whitewashed wall, squeezing his eyes shut tight as the beam of the headlights cut through the darkness and seared his brain. He waited for the car to pass, and for both the light and pain to recede.

Deker stepped cautiously into the deserted street and made his way down the sidewalk, concealing himself in doorways and behind hawkers' stands closed up for the night. They hadn't gone two blocks before he heard voices and smelled tobacco. Two men stood talking to each other, leaning against the wall of a darkened restaurant. And beyond them in the alley sat a black S-Class Mercedes.

"I've got the one on the left, you've got the one on the right," Deker said, his body going cold as they moved forward, the iron discipline of the IDF kicking in. He hit the guard on the left with a blow to the back and then across the Adam's apple. Elezar simply grabbed the head of the other guard and with a twist snapped his neck. Both men were on the ground without a sound.

Elezar lifted a phone off the driver and tossed Deker the car keys. "You drive!"

Deker threw open the driver's-side door and jumped behind the wheel, Elezar sliding in shotgun. Deker gunned the engine and shifted into drive, running over an empty fruit cart on the way out of the narrow alley. He switched on the headlights and swung by the roundabout, onto the main road heading north out of town.

3

Deker blew past the turnoff to Amman a mile outside Madaba and cut across the desert in the opposite direction, anxious to avoid roadblocks. In order to secure extraction, they had to contact the Israelis before they reached the Allenby Bridge at the Jordan River. But so far Elezar had no luck finding a wireless signal.

"You've got to let our side know we're coming," Deker said. "No private vehicles are allowed to cross the Allenby. We're as likely to die from Israeli bullets as Jordanian."

"I would if this Arab piece of shit worked." Elezar banged the phone he had lifted from the Jordanians against the dashboard. "Just drive."

Deker's mind, still a jumble of images from his torture, was racing faster than the stolen Mercedes. This mysterious Arab organization had penetrated the Waqf, perhaps now controlled it, and was planning to blow the Temple Mount. No doubt they would leave the Dome of the Rock standing and blame the failed attempt on Jewish extremists—specifically, him and Elezar. Riots would ensue and the Palestinians would declare Jerusalem, at least the Old City, as the capital of a new Palestine. Arab nations, and probably the Russians and Chinese, would instantly recognize the new nation, much as President Truman of the United States recognized the State of Israel in 1948. At that point, arms would flow into the new Palestine, further threatening Israel's existence and making it even more of an isolated fortress than it already was.

Unless the Tehown was activated.

But the legendary fail-safe required an artifact Israel did not officially possess, one that Deker had buried beneath the Temple Mount. And so far as Deker knew, the Tehown was more pedestrian than this cosmic gate or tunnel the Jordanian imagined. Now Deker was beginning to wonder if, in fact, he knew as much as he and his dead captors thought he did.

The speedometer showed 120 kilometers, but the Mercedes felt as if it was dragging. Or maybe it was the lingering effects of his torture. The flashes of light seemed burned into his retinas, as if he had stared into the sun too long. Even now, in the dead of night, he couldn't blink the brightness away. The needle marks on his arm also concerned him, and he wondered what sort of chemical cocktail was coursing through his veins.

Deker looked out his window and was at once both reassured and troubled to see the black cutout of Mount Nebo soaring above the Jordan Valley as they crossed into what in ancient times was known as the plains of Moab.

"Mount Nebo is where Moses viewed the Promised Land," Elezar lectured authoritatively, as he often did. "You can see the Jordan Valley, Jericho and the Judean hills beyond."

Deker had been to Nebo's summit with Rachel. The two of them used to hike the canyons of the Wadi Mujeb nature reserve off the King's Highway to the south. They had planned to come back one day.

"You know who Moses is, Deker, don't you?" Elezar asked with condescension in his voice.

Despite Deker's many demolitions and decorations in heroic service for Israel, Elezar had never considered him to be a "true Jew." That's because Deker grew up an American Jew on the coddled Westside of Los Angeles. Not like Elezar, twenty years his senior, who was raised in the Jewish settlements of the West Bank, knowing his family could be wiped out in an instant.

"Just because I'm not an observant Jew like you doesn't mean I'm entirely ignorant of our history, you self-righteous ass."

Deker long ago had lost patience with self-appointed holy warriors like Elezar. At one time the IDF was led by men like Deker: secular, Western and educated. Now it was controlled by religious nationalists like Elezar. But just because Elezar was anointed with oil by Brigadier General Avichai, the IDF's chief rabbi, and liked to wave the holy Torah around, it didn't make Elezar or his fellow former Golani Brigade officers the official representatives of the Jewish people.

"It's your ignorance that compromises the IDF," Elezar said. "How do I know that you're not the Black Dove?"

Deker bristled. The Black Dove was the code name for a suspected Hamas mole deep within the IDF. Until Rachel's death, Deker had always wondered if the IDF made up the Black Dove to justify all kinds of military operations against Hamas as well as periodic purges of undesirable officers within its ranks. But the Black Dove clearly knew enough about the IDF's plans to switch the bowl that Deker had crafted to assassinate him and senior Hamas officials. Later Deker suspected that Husseini, the Waqf official at the Temple Mount, might be the Black Dove, as he was someone whose position gave him access to both Israeli IDF and Jordanian GID personnel. That's what prompted him to conduct tonight's test of the Temple Mount. It was also why he almost killed Husseini when the bastard brought up Rachel's death and showed him a similar ceremonial washbowl like the one that killed her. In hindsight, perhaps he should have.

"So because I'm not a self-righteous ass like you, I'm a mythical Palestinian mole inside the IDF?" Deker asked, to expose the absurdity of Elezar's logic.

But Elezar was unrepentant. "You might as well be the Black Dove if they broke you."

"The only thing broken is your recording of these accusations that you insist on playing over and over," Deker replied. "You're not helping the situation."

Elezar was quiet for the next few minutes, except to occasionally curse his Jew-hating phone and blather in the darkness about the history of "God's people"—meaning himself.

Deker concentrated the best he could on the road as the highway expanded to two lanes both ways. He pressed the accelerator through the floor.

"Forget the phone: Get the guns," Deker said. "We're not stopping until this car skids to a halt on the other side of the Jordan like a block of Swiss cheese shot full of holes."

Deker peered through the windshield as they approached the bend in the highway, trying to sense how close they were. The Jordan River flowed down from the melting snow atop Mount Hermon in Lebanon to the Dead Sea. It was easy enough to pick out from satellite overheads, because it coursed two hundred kilometers through a tectonic fault zone known as the Great Rift Valley with its two plates on either side. But right here, right now, he couldn't see the river.

Deker scanned the night horizon for the first sign of the Allenby Border Terminal. Known as the King Hussein Bridge to Jordanians, the Allenby was the biggest of three bridges over the Jordan River connecting the country of Jordan to the Palestinian territories of the Israeli-controlled West Bank.

He began flashing distress signals in code with the headlights, but it was too late. Dead ahead was a line of Jordanian military trucks and police patrol cars blocking the road to the bridge.

"Roadblock!" Elezar shouted, leaning out the passenger-side window and firing bullets until he emptied his magazine.

No fire was returned. It wasn't necessary. Through his windshield Deker could see a thick nail strip across the freeway coming up fast, ready to blow their tires and stop them cold before they ever reached the roadblock.

Deker swung the wheel, scraping the nearside fender against the metal rail so that sparks flew. There was a thud, and then they were off the road, driving over the pocked and bumpy rock of the desert and covered in a cloud of sand and dust. The car skidded across the soil as Deker hit the accelerator, the tires chewing rocks and spitting them up against both sides of the car with loud pings.

"Ditch the car!" Elezar commanded.

The banks of the Jordan were coming up fast, even if Deker couldn't see them. As soon as he sensed the downward slope, he turned to Elezar and yelled, "Jump!"

Deker grabbed his combat bag from the backseat with one hand, kicked opened his door and dove out, hitting the rocky soil hard and tumbling several times as trained to lessen the impact. He was cut up everywhere, to be sure, and maybe even broke something. But now was the time to move, before the surge of adrenaline from the shock wore off.

"We go for the old footbridge," Deker said as he made his way across the moonscape, aware of Elezar stumbling alongside him, breathing heavily. Elezar didn't seem injured, but no matter how excellent his physical condition, the two additional decades he had on Deker weren't helping him here, and Deker easily beat him down the banks to the water.

But he couldn't find the footbridge. He looked up and down the winding waterway and couldn't find any bridge in the distance, including the Allenby.

"The bastards have blown the bridge!" Elezar raged. "They've started the attack! This is all your doing, Deker! If we survive this, I'll have you executed for treason!"

"Then at least I'll be executed by Jews," Deker said, unmoved. "We have to swim for it."

Deker lifted his pack onto his shoulder and descended the banks to the river until he felt the cold water around his ankles. Agriculture over the decades had drained the Jordan of whatever depth and current it might have possessed in ancient days. He couldn't see the other side in the dark. But the distance was probably less than seven meters across, and the depth in some places less than one.

"Elezar—"

But there was no reply. He glanced over his shoulder at Elezar, crumpled on the ground. He looked up the embankment at five black figures cut out against the stars. He turned to dive into the water when he felt a searing stab in his back.

He reached behind, yanked an object out and brought it before his eyes. It was a spear. He stared in confusion and dismay at the large, leaf-shaped spearhead, like something from the Bronze Age exhibit at the Israel Museum in Jerusalem.

He saw the black stain on the tip in the moonlight and realized he was losing blood fast. His eyes began to blur as he watched the spearhead fall in slow motion from his hands. Then he felt himself lurch forward and tumble into the cold, dark waters of the Jordan.

4

Seated inside the airy temple in Los Angeles for his bar mitzvah, his family and friends smiled through tears as the rabbi reached into the open Ark and handed him the Torah scroll containing the Five Books of Moses.

It was one of the older Torahs, weighing almost fifty pounds, and he struggled to carry it in his slender, trembling hands. It felt like a boulder. He was thirteen and considered a man now according to Jewish tradition. But he was still a year away from his growth spurt, and his tired arms weren't strong enough to carry it.

As he tried to balance the Torah, it began to tip. There were gasps from the adults and a snicker or two from the children. *Oh, no! The Holy Law!* He tried to right it but overcompensated. *I can't hold it! It's slipping!* Like a dream he watched it fall from his hands, just beyond his fingertips, until it hit the platform with a crash and split open.

Deker woke from his childhood memory into the searing light of day. He felt the hot desert wind blow and heard the rustling of leaves. The scent of flowers was sweet, but it couldn't mask something foul in the air.

He blinked his eyes open and tried to move but couldn't. His legs and arms seemed locked. Then he realized he was naked and wrapped around the golden bark of a seven-meter-tall acacia tree. His right leg was bent around the front of the tree and locked inside his bent left leg, which in turn was locked behind the trunk under the entire weight of his own body. They were using the "grapevine" method to secure him as a prisoner. Very old-school, but effective.

He was in some kind of grove of acacia trees, gnarly and black against the sky, their green and yellow leaves blowing like ash in the air.

Pain shot up his spine from the cramping in both his legs. *How long have I been left like this?* He dug his fingers into the tree trunk and tried to pull himself up. His skin scraped against the bark and he moved up only enough for his head to scratch the sharp thorns of the lower branches. He had an overwhelming desire to throw himself backward to relieve the unbearable pain. But somehow his body sensed that such an action would kill him.

He lifted his head and scanned the grove. It took a moment for his eyes to adjust to the brightness. He couldn't make out the strange black limbs of the golden trees. Then he realized they were rotting human limbs, blackened by the sun. The ash in the air was but flecks of charred flesh carried in the wind.

Horrified, he looked up into the branches above him and saw a half-rotten, sunken face staring at him with pecked-out eyes.

Unable to tear his eyes away, he stared back for a moment, a moan unable to take form at the back of his parched throat. All around him were thousands of corpses strung up in the trees, slits of sunlight shining through their perforated torsos, their mouths open in twisted screams.

He looked away and his throat began to convulse to vomit. But nothing came out. Once, twice, his wrung-out body seemed to constrict from the inside out like a dry, twisted rag around the tree.

This was some kind of mass grave, a grove of the dead. Except the genocidal maniacs who had done this hadn't bothered to bury the bodies, preferring to string them up instead as a warning to somebody.

Suddenly, several shadows blocked the light and he heard a voice in garbled Hebrew say something like "Clean him up."

A thin hyssop branch with narrow blue leaves was waved in front of his face and he felt the cool sprinkle of some kind of aromatic water.

The drops of water on his dry tongue only awakened his senses, and he could taste a fleck of ash.

He tried to spit it out but could manage only a dry groan as several shadows lifted him up and dragged him away from the tree and propped him up against a low stone wall, where his weak legs could barely keep him upright.

In the distance Mount Nebo lifted into the sky under the blazing sun. He blinked. By all appearances he was still somewhere in Jordan. But something didn't feel right, and it wasn't just his personal predicament. Something greater had shifted around him, and the jarring sense of reality shook him to his core.

His nightmare, he realized, had only just begun.

5

Deker was doused with jars of water several times over before he was dragged naked into a desert tent. The tent itself was large and austere, with only a rough-hewn table on which he saw a ceramic jug and bowl—and the contents of his explosives pack neatly laid in a row. Everything about the place seemed washed-out, as though he were looking at the world through some sepia-tinted filter.

Deker was tied to one of two posts that supported the tent. Elezar was tied to the other. His head drooped. He seemed unconscious, and Deker saw bruises and cuts. He couldn't tell if they were from the night before or new ones. Then he wondered about the spear he had pulled out of his own back as he slid uncomfortably against his post.

A blast of heat blew in as the tent flap opened wide to reveal a sea of similar tents in the sands outside. It was a sight Deker had seen before in the Palestinian refugee camps of Gaza and the West Bank. The same for the haunted faces of the two young soldiers who entered and stood before him in all their muscularity.

Palestinians, he could only presume.

"Where the hell am I?" Deker demanded in English. "What did you do to those people?"

The big, strapping, swarthy guard, who carried a giant bronze sickle sword on his rope belt for effect, glanced over at his smaller, towheaded comrade, a confused look on his face, as if he didn't understand the prisoner.

Deker tried Arabic. "Who the hell are you?"

The big Palestinian answered by slamming Deker's head against the pole. Deker felt a splinter in his forehead and a trickle of blood run down his cheek.

"Who are you, spy?" the Palestinian demanded in bad Hebrew. At least, it sounded like Hebrew. "How did you sneak into our camp?"

"Say nothing, Deker."

It was Elezar come to life, a strange look on his face.

The big Palestinian moved toward the table, on which were laid Deker's BlackBerry and explosives. He picked up the BlackBerry, fascinated. "Where did you get these?"

"Toys 'R' Us," Deker replied, this time getting a firm whack on the back of the head from the other guard.

The big guard pressed some buttons and somehow accessed the music player. The music of "Learn to Fly" by the Foo Fighters blasted out, startling the guard. He dropped the BlackBerry on the table and smashed it to pieces.

Deker sighed and locked onto the water that splashed out of the ceramic pot on the table when the guard smashed the phone. Deker's mind immediately went to work on how to escape—after a drink from that pitcher. He licked his dry, parched lips. Just a drop to quench the thirst, he thought, when the flap to the tent fluttered again.

A lean, wiry, gray-bearded figure in a strange military outfit entered the tent, followed by a short, fat man in a white priestly garment whom Deker recognized as the one who had sprinkled his face with water and ash back in the death grove.

"General Bin-Nun!" the guards saluted.

Deker saw Elezar's jaw drop.

A walking piece of bronze in his sixties, this General Bin-Nun had a leathery face with hollow cheeks and wild blue eyes with a far-off gaze. A zealot, in other words. The look was typical of tribal chiefs and desert warlords in the Middle East. But Deker did not recognize the man behind the grey beard. Nor the strange body armor and scimitar sword he was sporting, which gave him the ghastly air of some Afghan warlord in a pharaoh's armor.

Elezar, however, looked like he had seen a ghost.

Deker watched as Bin-Nun walked around to the table and examined the weapons. He looked at the pieces of the smashed BlackBerry and shot an angry glance at the big guard, who looked down at the ground. Then he picked up a brick of C-4 and put it down again. He seemed particularly interested in the look and feel of the detonators.

"Send these over to Kane," Bin-Nun told the big guard in the same type of bad Hebrew the guard had used on Deker. It rang familiar enough for him to understand, but just barely, like a strange brew of ancient and modern Hebrew with an exotic, almost Egyptian accent.

The general then turned to Deker, leaning over inches from Deker's face. Deker could feel his penetrating glare linger before the general's eyes widened with the shock of recognition at the Star of David around Deker's neck. It was not a pleasant reaction.

"They are Reahns, General," the short, fat priest said. He looked like an evil cherub, the way his face sneered as he spoke. "They bear the blazing star. They belong to the cult of Molech. They bow to the same god as the calf worshipers who brought the wrath of Moses upon us."

"But they are cut like us, Phineas."

Deker, thoroughly confused now, realized they were talking about his circumcised penis. He could see Bin-Nun making some sort of mental calculation as he curiously considered his two naked prisoners.

"They must die," Phineas said, glaring at Deker. "Moses would—"

"Moses is dead," Bin-Nun said, cutting off the priest.

Deker heard the unmistakable swish of a blade and looked up to see the general bring the scimitar down, stopping at the last moment an inch above Deker's skull.

The general spoke harshly, too fast for Deker to understand.

"What's he saying?" Deker asked Elezar in English, prompting the warlord's guards to exchange confused glances. As a political officer, Elezar was fluent in the history and languages of the Middle East.

"It's ancient Hebrew," Elezar said haltingly. "He wants to know if we're for them or against them."

Deker said, "We don't even know who the hell these people are."

"These are Jews." There was a hint of fear in Elezar's voice as he looked around, a worrisome sign to Deker. "This is Joshua, the son of Nun, general of the ancient Israelite army. Somehow we have arrived at their camp in Shittim on the eve of their historic siege of Jericho more than three thousand years ago."

Deker stared at his superior officer. Somewhere during their torture, escape and recapture, something must have snapped in his head.

"They are not Jews, Elezar," Deker said patiently, aware of the sharp edge of the sword on his skull. "This bastard is not Joshua of the Hebrew Bible come to life, and we have not gone back in time."

Elezar cleared his throat and gave a reply in the same exotic dialect as this "General Bin-Nun," although Deker understood the unmistakable name of Adonai only at the end.

To Deker's amazement, Bin-Nun withdrew his sword and said something else to Elezar and the guards before he marched out of the tent.

"What did you say to him?" Deker demanded as the two guards eased them up and brought them outside the tent.

"I said we're neither for him nor against him," Elezar said, blinking into the sun beneath his sweaty brow. "We're angels in the army of the Lord."

"What?" Deker stared at the sea of black acacia trees to the south and a sea of white tents to the north, the land of the dead versus the land of the living. "And what did he say?"

"Prove it, or we can rot out there with the rest of the damned."

6

Deker and Elezar, wearing simple beige tunics, were marched barefoot across the hot sands of the camp toward a towering pillar of smoke in the east. The most striking thing about this city of otherwise weather-beaten tents was how pristine and full of life it was after the filth and stench of the death grove they had left behind.

Deker strained to look beyond the first row or two of tents into the encampment. The population was young—very young—like so many of the Palestinian camps, including plenty of pregnant girls who looked barely in their teens. Other than General Bin-Nun, Deker didn't see anybody older than thirty. Not a wrinkle in sight.

"This camp isn't on any of our maps," Deker said in English.

"Of course not, Deker," Elezar said excitedly. "This is Shittim. It means the 'Meadow of the Acacias.' That's what all those trees were back there. Shittimwood is what the ancient Israelites used to build the Ark of the Covenant and the desert Tabernacle. This is a miracle."

"What the hell are you talking about?" Deker said with a glance back as the spears from their armed escort prodded them forward. The soldiers either didn't understand English or didn't care if they talked. "You call that mass grave we saw back there a miracle?"

"What kind of Israeli soldier are you, to be so ignorant of history?" Elezar scolded him. "Those are the twenty-four thousand Israelites whom Moses ordered slaughtered by the Levite priests shortly before he died. Probably only a month or two ago since the camp seems to be coming off its official period of mourning."

"Israelites? Moses?" Deker couldn't believe his ears. "Do you hear yourself?"

"Yes, but do you, Deker? Because you might want to listen up if you want to live," Elezar shot back. "The Israelites only recently pitched camp here after forty years in the desert. As soon as they did, a lot of the soldiers started screwing around with the local Moabite and Midianite women. Yahweh—that's God, in case you forgot— then threatened judgment on Israel. So Phineas the Levite, that priest who sprinkled us with holy water back at the grove, picked up a spear and ran it through an Israelite man and Midianite woman while they were in the act. That inspired Moses and the rest of the Levites to pick up the sword and slaughter the rest. We're living ancient history."

"Whatever you call that back there, Elezar, I call it a war crime," Deker told him. "Possibly genocide. At the very least a crime against humanity."

"Your moral outrage only reveals your ignorance," Elezar said. "Obviously, sexually transmitted diseases were thinning the ranks of the army on the eve of its invasion of the Promised Land. The slaughter saved the entire Israelite camp here. The sooner you accept our new reality, Deker, the sooner we can deal with it."

"Bullshit," Deker said. "And this is a Palestinian camp. A terrorist camp."

"Look around you, Deker," Elezar pressed. "This camp is laid out in four sections, each section divided into three tribes. Just like the ancient Israelites pitched their camps. See those Manasseh archers and Benjaminite slingers to our west? That's the Ephraim Division. And those light infantry divisions to our south? Those are the tribes of Reuben, Gad and Simeon."

Deker noted all the long spears, sickle swords, bows, slings and shields Elezar was pointing out. True, he saw no AK-47 rifles, no grenade launchers, not even a cell phone. But throw in a couple of satellite dishes and this camp would look right at home in the twenty-first century.

"This camp is too advanced to be the ancient Israelite camp," Deker announced. "They've got their latrines on one side of the camp, near the decontamination tents we came out of, and their natural water supply on the other. Armies didn't have this kind of sanitation until World War I. It's like spotting a digital watch on the wrist of a Roman centurion in some Hollywood swords-and-sandals epic."

"What are you suggesting?" Elezar pressed, clearly anticipating a response he would easily dismiss with the irrefutable logic of his inherent seniority, which he equated with superiority.

"Maybe this camp is some sort of movie studio back lot disguised to throw us off," he suggested, trying to reason in some way with Elezar, to bring him back to the cold reality. Otherwise, he'd have to attempt to escape on his own. "Maybe the real terrorists and their weapons are hiding somewhere. We just can't see them."

"We can't see any vapor trails, either, Deker. Have they changed the skies too? It's been at least ten minutes and not even the distant sound of a warplane."

Which was true, Deker thought, as he glanced up at the white-hot sky. There was stillness in the air here. It lent an otherworldly quality to everything he was now experiencing through his physical senses.

"Maybe we're not anywhere," he finally said. "Maybe we're still strapped in some Jordanian dungeon somewhere, suffering from some torture-induced psychosis. Or maybe we're dead."

From Elezar's reaction, it was clear to Deker that his superior refused to even entertain the notion of his own mortality, let alone waking up in the same afterlife as his secular, American-born, bad Jew-boy underling.

"We're not dead, Deker. And the two of us both can't be in the same psychosis."

"So instead you're suggesting we're time travelers?"

"I'm suggesting we've traveled through time," Elezar said, now passing himself off as a lay physicist as well as a Talmud scholar. "Space-time is like a flat surface. When it's curved or bent back on itself like a wrinkle, it creates a 'wormhole' that connects one part of space-time to another. In our case, the wormhole connects our 'present day' in the future to the here and now of 1400 BC in a closed loop. You know how past, present and future seem to collide every day around Jerusalem, Deker, and throughout this part of the world. For all we know, this is the true Tehown, or cosmic 'tunnel of chaos,' that this mysterious Waqf splinter group has been after for centuries."

It was almost too much for Deker's brain to process. "To what end, Elezar?"

"Obviously, to erase Israel from history before it ever becomes a nation," Elezar said, visibly perturbed that Deker was still playing catch-up with his reality.

Deker closed his eyes as they walked. He felt the burning sand beneath the soles of his feet. They were beginning to blister. He could hear the sounds of children at play, hammers and saws and shouts in the distance. He could smell the fragrance of desert flowers. Finally, he could still taste that burnt ash on his tongue from the death grove.

"So if we're not dead, and we're not hallucinating, and this truly is Camp Shittim some three thousand years back in time," Deker said as he opened his eyes, "then where's the Ark of the Covenant?"

"Over there," Elezar said excitedly, pointing out a large white tent that stood out from the others. "That's the Tent of Meeting. You know what's in there, Deker, don't you?"

"A stolen Soviet nuke?"

"The Ark!" Elezar was beside himself now, clearly dying to take a peek inside the Tent of Meeting. He cleared his throat and addressed their two escorts in ancient Hebrew. "Can we see inside?"

The guards looked to where Elezar was pointing and then glanced at each other. The big one snorted. Even Deker could understand it meant *In your dreams.*

Deker said, "Well, maybe you can at least explain what that column of smoke is up ahead. The burning bush?"

"Close," Elezar told him solemnly. "It's the very presence of God."

"Have it your way, Elezar, but we're damned if these are Palestinians and damned if they're ancient Jews. Because in case you haven't noticed from the spears at our backs, even a Super Jew like you doesn't make the grade with these fanatics."

7

The presence of God turned out to be a twenty-meter-tall signal tower made of shittimwood beams with ladders leading to its various levels, all building up to a bronze furnace and chimney. It was manned by a contingent of soldiers who stoked it while an officer barked orders.

Deker was tempted to taunt Elezar with some joke about how many priests Yahweh needed to screw in a lightbulb. But as ordinary as these pyrotechnics turned out to be, the entire scene was still all too extraordinary for him.

"And we're the ones who have to prove ourselves?" Deker told a dismayed Elezar. "So much for seeing Yahweh."

"So much for your Palestinian camp, Deker," Elezar countered. "With a column of smoke like that, the IDF wouldn't need a satellite to know of this camp's existence. You could stand on the Temple Mount in Jerusalem and see this cloud."

Which was true, Deker thought as a large group of military officers now entered the clearing behind Bin-Nun. He counted forty of them, in addition to four priests and an older man, only the second Deker had seen so far, counting Bin-Nun.

"If each commander represents two hundred troops—the equivalent of an IDF combat unit—that puts Bin-Nun's troop levels at eight thousand," Deker whispered to Elezar. "If the ancient one-to-four ratio holds and the troops comprise a quarter of the general population, then we're talking a bit more than thirty thousand Israelites total. Not quite the 2.5 million I recall from Hebrew school."

"I knew," Elezar said, revealing some distress.

That in turn distressed Deker, because it meant that Elezar truly believed they were back in biblical times, and that this "reality" didn't jibe with his preconceived notions.

Deker watched as General Bin-Nun consulted with the other old-timer, who pointed toward a stone monument about a hundred meters away. Bin-Nun nodded, and the group migrated over to what looked like a gigantic stone table but which Deker recognized as a Neolithic dolmen, a flat megalith laid across shorter stones to mark an ancient tomb.

This dolmen was ancient even by ancient standards. Its horizontal capstone ran four meters long and two meters wide. Each of the three upright stones supporting it was about a meter tall. At one time there had been a mound of dirt covering the tomb, but the winds of history had stripped it away, and all that remained was the skeleton of stones.

Here the commanders gathered in a semicircle around the two of them, and for a crazy moment Deker worried they were going to be stoned and buried under the dolmen. Instead, the other old man came forward with Deker's pack of explosives.

Deker snatched them while the old man spoke to Elezar.

"Kane is the head of the Israelites' arsenal," Elezar told Deker afterward. "Their chief weapons procurer. Swords, spears and all that. He's a Kenite and a cousin of Moses. Basically an arms dealer who trades in metals and manufactures the weapons of Joshua's army. He joined up with the Israelites after the Exodus when Joshua was first starting to breed his army for Moses. He can't reverse-engineer what he's calling our 'magic mud bricks,' but he knows from the blinking timers that they're not of this world, and the slight odor of elemental sulfur in the bricks suggests that they possess the same properties as whatever Yahweh's angels used to destroy Sodom and Gomorrah. So Bin-Nun wants you to demonstrate their power. He wants you to destroy the dolmen."

Deker paused. "This would be the first bomb I set off since Rachel."

"Yes," Elezar said. "And you'll do it to save your life and mine."

Deker looked at Elezar. "And take out the Israelite high command here in one strike so we can escape?"

Elezar looked at him coldly. "See those eight commanders over there with the purple tassels on their breastplates branded with the sign of Gemini?"

"What about them?"

"Tribe of Benjamin. Isn't that the tribe of your family's ancestry? Kill them all here and you'll have never been born. Neither you, nor I, nor the nation of Israel."

"You're as crazy as these fanatics," Deker said, clutching his C-4 bricks. "To escape, we'd have to kill our captors. But you're saying if we kill our captors, we might not only kill ourselves but all Israel."

As he spoke, he could feel old Kane and the group of command-ers studying with keen interest how he handled the C-4. It was the digital displays on the timers that seemed to captivate his audience, not the "magic mud bricks" themselves. They mistakenly thought the power resided in the timers, not in the C-4. They obviously had no clue that the kill zone of a single brick was almost twenty-five meters and that nothing or nobody could survive inside that circle.

For the first time he was afraid there might be something to Elezar's insane idea that they had gone back in time. These people seemed to have absolutely no clue as to the destructive power of this stuff. That was impossible in the twenty-first century. Even the most backward camp in the Middle East had a bomb maker, if nothing else.

Elezar said, "Just prove we're angels of the Lord, Deker, and maybe we can escape this . . . place."

Deker looked over his shoulder at the dolmen monument behind them. "I don't like it. I have no idea how it's going to break up or where the pieces will fly. Might take us out with them. How about a fire in the hole, a pillar of fire?"

Elezar repeated this to Kane, who shook his head.

"They have a pillar of fire," Elezar said, noting the column of smoke. "They want you to vaporize the stone."

Deker carefully inspected the dolmen he was about to blow sky-high. The three supporting stones were sandstone, the capstone travertine. He'd have to direct the blast to flip the top away from the viewing parade of commanders before it broke up.

His true gift, as Husseini had implied back at the Temple Mount, was his ability to locate in a structure the precise "pressure point" to bring the whole thing down with just the tiniest nudge. A building. A dam. It didn't matter. Deker was a demolition black belt who used his target's own weight against itself.

As he leaned over and got to work with a single C-4 brick, he could feel old Kane breathing over his shoulder, watching him ply the putty into a natural sandstone groove halfway up one of the supporting boulders.

This is going to be sloppy, Deker realized, but he had no time to prep the stone or anchor the brick properly. This was supposed to be magic, after all: fire from heaven. Too much preparation would reflect poorly on Yahweh's angels.

Moreover, since their lives were on the line, he would have to risk overkill and a flair for the dramatic by throwing in another brick for good measure: one brick of C-4 to blow out one leg with a short timer, and then a second brick on a slightly longer timer to push and twist the monument's capstone up and out in the proper direction—away from his alleged ancestors.

Bricks lodged and smoothed into place, Deker inserted the twin blast pins with radio receivers deep into each clump of putty. He set the timers just a millisecond apart. The green light on each pin detonator began to blink, signaling that its explosive was armed.

Taking a look at what his hands had so quickly wrought, Deker suddenly worried that Kane and the rest weren't far enough away.

"Get them back, Elezar!" he shouted.

Elezar began yelling as Deker ran toward the signal tower,

most of the others in tow. But Kane, arms folded, remained standing a few meters away, refusing to look panicked or concerned.

Damn it, Deker thought, and ran back to the old man and dragged him away from the stone monument.

Stay here! he signaled with his left palm out.

Deker raised his arms to the sky like Moses for dramatic effect, tightening his grip around the wireless pen-shaped detonator in his right hand. His thumb rested on the red button on top. He pumped once, releasing the safety. Then he pumped again, sending a radio signal to the receivers embedded in the C-4.

There was a split-second delay, then a one-two blast that blew up the capstone. The shock wave blew him back off his feet and sent the line of commanders behind him to their knees, where they clapped their ears under their helmets. Meanwhile, broken pieces of rock exploded in the opposite direction.

Deker, ears ringing, felt the ground shake as the boulders bashed each other to bits and came raining down hard, raising a cloud of dust and debris into the air.

He coughed twice and helped the smiling old Kane up to his feet. If the guy wasn't deaf before, he probably was now.

Everybody else removed their hands from their ears. A few went wobbly in the legs, having trouble with their balance. All were staring at the small pieces of rock scattered across the ground.

It was suddenly quiet again, save for the howls from a few boys who had secretly sneaked out for the show.

General Bin-Nun suddenly threw his hands up to heaven and shouted, *"Kol han-nesama!"*

Hope had returned to his haunted eyes with the explosion,

and Deker could see a glint of genuine relief in his face as the rest began to chant after him.

"*Kol han-nesama! Kol han-nesama! Kol han-nesama!*"

But the shouts to heaven had wiped the smiles off the faces of Phineas and the Levites, who looked at Deker like he was the devil.

"*Kol han-nesama! Kol han-nesama! Kol han-nesama!*"

"What are they saying?" Deker called to Elezar.

Elezar, his eyes ablaze with joy, said, "It means 'Every breathing thing.'"

"What does *that* mean?"

"Bin-Nun has declared a holy war. They're calling for death to everything that breathes."

Deker had a sinking feeling. "What about us?"

"He says we're free to return to heaven," Elezar answered. "Just as soon as we spy out Jericho and come back and tell them how to blow up its walls."

8

At sundown Deker stood in the clearing where he had blown up the dolmen monument and watched the column of smoke atop the signal tower turn into a pillar of fire. The change announced the start of a new day on the Hebrew calendar along with his and Elezar's mission to spy out Jericho.

Ancient Israelites. General Joshua bin-Nun. The Promised Land. Yahweh.

None of it made any sense. All he knew was that he wanted to cross the Jordan River and enter the Israeli-occupied West Bank territories and escape this nightmare. The shouts of the commanders from that afternoon were still ringing in his ears.

Every breathing thing. Every thing that breathes.

Deker scratched at his itchy change of clothing, which included a long-sleeved gray cashmere shirt, tight-fitting brown-burgundy wool pants and white deerskin boots. He couldn't wait to see Elezar's getup when his superior finally emerged from the nearby changing tent.

Standing by to bless them on their way was Phineas the Levite. The young, fat priest actually seemed sorry to see him go.

"You and the angel Elezar appeared and gave Bin-Nun his first miracle today," Phineas told him in ancient Hebrew while he stood before the signal tower.

Deker was beginning to understand his ancestral tongue after hearing it spoken over his cattle-and-corn dinner, most of the talking coming from Phineas. The priest's monologues were longer than Elezar's. Speaking ancient Hebrew, however, would be a challenge, one Deker hoped would be wholly unnecessary as soon as he and Elezar were off.

"He needed a sign of Yahweh's blessing on him as Moses had," Phineas went on about General Bin-Nun, seemingly unaware that the halo effect of the pillar of fire behind him lent him a rather hellish aura. "He seems to have found it with you and your magic mud bricks. He'll need more signs and wonders to lead us into the Promised Land."

Apparently so, Deker realized, what with the likes of Phineas and the rest of the Levites whom General Bin-Nun had to deal with. They obviously had served as Moses' own sort of Praetorian Guards until Bin-Nun wisely disarmed them upon assuming command of not only the army but also the nation, such as it was. Still, Bin-Nun had to assuage the clergy. Especially now, as they prepared to cross the Jordan River into the land they claimed God had promised their forefather Abraham.

"The manna grain that has fed us for forty years is drying up,

and the troops have resorted to grabbing food by attacking cara-
vans on the King's Highway to the east," Phineas confided in him.
"The sooner we reach the land of milk and honey, the better for
us all."

If food was in short supply, Phineas certainly didn't look like
he was suffering as he lovingly used a stone to sharpen the bronze
tip of his spear like a pool cue. It was the same spear, he had
boasted earlier, that he had used to shish-kebab the Midianite
princess Cozbi and her Hebrew backslider in mid-fornication.
He took particular pride in demonstrating the motion of his single thrust through the back of the Hebrew and into the belly of
the Midianite. He even hazarded a hope that she had been with
child, although he confessed she would have been too early in
her term to be certain.

Deker nodded at Phineas as Elezar at last appeared with
Salmon and Achan, the young Judah Division guards who had
welcomed them into Camp Shittim by hosing them down and
whacking them around the decontamination tent.

Elezar had the horses and supplies, along with his equally hid-
eous change of clothing: a long-sleeved tan cashmere shirt, close-
cropped olive wool pants and white deerskin boots.

"What the hell is going on, Elezar?" Deker demanded as they
mounted their horses. "We look like pimps from Tel Aviv."

"The book of Joshua in the Hebrew scriptures says that Joshua
the son of Nun sent two spies from Shittim to Jericho in advance
of the invasion."

"Surely their names weren't Deker and Elezar."

"Scripture mysteriously doesn't say," Elezar answered him. "But we have no choice except to play along and hopefully cross the Jordan to our time."

What a strange idea, Deker thought. But he said nothing as Phineas blessed their horses with his branch and holy water, said his prayer for the success of the *jihad*-obsessed Israelite army and waved them off.

9

It took forty minutes on horseback in the dark to reach the secret Israelite river base. They secured their horses and gathered around a stone table illuminated by several oil lamps. It was a dolmen capstone almost twenty feet long, conscripted to serve the base as combination outdoor mess hall and operations center.

Deker couldn't see the Jordan, but he could hear the river's waters just beyond the tents and wood sheds. He also heard some rustling in the bushes, and out came the man they had come to see with a parchment rolled under his arm.

The big Judah Division soldier, Salmon, immediately greeted his hero. "Caleb," said Salmon. "Last of the old ones."

"You'll get there, son," Caleb said, glancing at Deker and Elezar. "If our friends here don't fail us."

Caleb was nearly as tall as Bin-Nun, with deeply tanned and weathered skin. His clothing was different than that of the tribal commanders—he wore no body armor or sword—and he had a quieter air about him than General Bin-Nun or Kane the Kenite.

But his flint-sharp, probing eyes seemed to miss nothing, and he clearly commanded the same respect as the two other "old ones" with the Israelite army's rank and file.

Caleb unrolled the parchment beneath the flicker of the oil lamps. It was a map of Canaan, the "Promised Land" to the ancient Hebrews, which would later be called Palestine and which Deker knew as modern-day Israel.

Caleb then stretched a long, muscular finger, flecked with age spots, over the map. He pointed to a city about four kilometers away on the other side of the Jordan. It was bounded by Mount Nebo to the east, the Central Mountains to the west and the Dead Sea to the south.

"Jericho," he said. "'City of the Moon.' Its Hivite inhabitants call it Reah, and themselves Reahns. Its strategic location allows it to control the trade routes through many cities of Canaan. As a result, Jericho is the perfect base from which to destroy or capture enemy convoys. Unfortunately, there is no way to conquer Canaan without first taking out Jericho. And we can't take out Jericho without destroying her walls."

Caleb looked up from the map, first at Elezar and then with unblinking eyes at Deker, holding his gaze until he seemed sure that Deker fully felt the essence of his mission: namely, that he and Elezar were to spy out the area, infiltrate Jericho's defenses and blow up the walls. Because, come hell or high water, tens of thousands of Israelites were going to invade the Promised Land.

"Then give me my magic mud bricks," Deker said in halfway decent ancient Hebrew and with his own unblinking gaze. "We'll be on our way."

But Caleb, who understood him perfectly, eyed him coldly. "No magic mud bricks. You are to spy out Jericho and come back with a report first."

"Only a report?"

Deker looked at Elezar for some help here. But Elezar responded only with a pained look on his face. Now was not the time to show off fluency in ancient tongues, his expression implied, or question orders, or do anything to delay their crossing.

"We'll want several plausible lines of march to the city," Caleb said, speaking directly to Elezar now, peer to peer. "And a full assessment of the fortifications and walls. Any weaknesses? Any way under or over? Most important, we need you to gauge the morale of the people of Jericho, especially her troops. They're now under the command of an Egyptian mercenary, General Hamas."

"Hamas?" Elezar said out loud with a start, echoing Deker's thoughts.

"You've heard of him, then?" Caleb said. "An evil monster who executes any officer who fails him with his own blade, but only after he feeds their children to Molech before their eyes."

"What's the king's name?" Deker asked Elezar directly in English. "Hezbollah?"

Elezar frowned at Deker, but Caleb seemed to pick up the gist of the question.

"Alakh is the provisional king," Caleb said. "It is said Hamas dispatched the king before him, and the one before him too. There is no royal family, only wealthy landowners whose taxes secure the troops who defend their holdings."

Deker heard a grunt from behind as Salmon, seeing their utter ignorance of the region's geopolitics, leaned over to Achan and quipped, "Angels of the Lord."

Caleb then handed Elezar a folded piece of papyrus. "One of our spies, before he died, intercepted this for us on the trade routes. It's a communiqué from Hamas to the kings of southern Canaan."

Elezar translated the text for Deker. "Hamas is asking local city-states for a consignment of the following weapons: 3,000 bows, 1,500 daggers, 1,500 swords and 50 additional chariots," Elezar told him in English.

"Sounds like he knows Yahweh is coming," Deker said.

Caleb said, "That's enough weapons to equip six thousand troops, more than twice the daytime population of Jericho and almost ten times the number of its men in uniform."

"But he's not asking for troops," said Elezar, handing the scroll back to Caleb. "Just weapons."

"So, where is Hamas finding the extra bodies?" Deker asked.

"Something else for you to find out," Caleb said. "There are rumors that Hamas has some kind of shadow army of demons ready to wipe out any invader who breaches Jericho's walls."

A shadow army, thought Deker, suddenly on alert. It sounded suspiciously similar to the phrase *legion of demons* that his superiors in the IDF often used to refer to the secret fail-safe he had buried beneath the Temple Mount in Jerusalem. Like Jericho's so-called shadow army, the Israeli fail-safe was a weapon of last resort, the ultimate self-destruct mechanism that would wipe out Jews and Arabs alike but ultimately ensure the survival of Israel.

The Israeli demons were contained inside a replica of the Ark of the Covenant that the IDF had code-named "Pandora's Box." Deker once knew what exactly was inside the box, before military hypnotherapists inflicted reverse-regression treatments on him to make him forget what he had buried. Indeed, the only image or feeling that he still could recall about the fail-safe was that it was very ancient. He also suspected it was a bioweapon of some sort. But such a device would be well beyond what General Hamas and the armies of Jericho were capable of developing.

Suddenly, Deker felt self-conscious of his thoughts, worried that he shouldn't even be thinking about the Israeli fail-safe or acknowledging to himself that it even existed.

For a split second Deker wondered if the wall of time and space was as porous as Elezar thought, and his sixth sense tingled, as though he had spotted a glitch in the universe. Then it was gone and he wondered if he had sensed anything at all.

I have to get back to Jerusalem, he reminded himself. *Have to stop the attack and prevent a wider war.*

"Deker!" said Elezar, breaking his trance. "Pay attention."

Deker refocused his eyes as Caleb presented him with a couple of thin bronze tags: passports of some sort, it appeared. The Israelite veteran then unrolled a long leather strip with jewelry and amulets pinned inside. Two more wraps sat on the stone table.

Young Achan let out a low whistle.

It was quite understandable. Deker figured there was probably two or three million U.S. dollars' worth of gems and precious metals in those jewelry wraps, and it made him wonder if he and Elezar were really going to walk out of there alive.

"You cross the Jordan tonight dressed as jewelry traders from the east. Kane the Kenite has prepared your cover here with passports and jewelry. Before daybreak, you will cut through the barley fields and olive groves on the other side of the Jordan. The road to Jericho is wide and well traveled. Hamas has reconnaissance chariots that regularly patrol it. You will join the road after the last checkpoint to Jericho, so that the main gate will be your one and only inspection. If you pass, you're in."

Elezar nodded, and it seemed they were done. But then Salmon slammed his fist on the stone table.

"This is not the plan," he nearly shouted at Caleb, the words hanging in the night air. "Achan and I were supposed to cross the Jordan and join the barley workers, bring the harvest through the gates of Jericho, spy it out and come back."

"Yahweh works in mysterious ways, Salmon," Deker said, and helped himself to the two other wraps, tucking them inside the folds of his tunic.

Caleb sighed and looked at Salmon. "It is what it is."

Deker then noticed one last little leather pouch that old Caleb fingered under his weathered hand. "What's that?"

Caleb opened the pouch with great care and presented him with a necklace with a silver pendant in the shape of a crescent moon. "If you get into trouble, you can go to Rahab's Inn," he said. "Give her this."

Deker picked up the necklace by the chain and looked at the crescent moon, the light from the oil lamps dancing like fire across its shiny surface. He watched Caleb's eyes follow his hand as he carefully put the necklace around his neck next to his IDF tag.

"She's the whore from the story, isn't she?" he asked Elezar in

English, trying to recall the details of the book of Joshua, if only to prove Hebrew school wasn't a complete waste of his parents' money.

"And older than I am, according to tradition," Elezar shot back, and then addressed Caleb. "It won't be necessary. We'll be out before the gate closes and return the necklace to you as you have given it to us now."

"That's probably best," Caleb said resolutely. "There's nobody better informed about the guard placements and shifts than the women who service those guards. But they cannot be trusted and may turn you over to be killed. Avoid Rahab's if you can, then, and bring the necklace back to me."

Deker nodded and then put his hand to Elezar's back. "Bribes, whores and deception," he said cynically, pushing Elezar forward to get out of there. "The work of Yahweh must go on."

10

The Jordan was a stone's throw away from the base, so a sullen Salmon and curious Achan walked Deker and Elezar over to its swollen banks to see them off. Deker's heart sank as soon as he saw the silvery surface ripple under the new moon. It had to be a kilometer across—a virtual impossibility in the twenty-first century, even if Palestinians had blown up every dam.

"Remember, it's shallower in the center," Achan offered, sensing Deker's concern but misunderstanding its origin. "Only three or four cubits deep."

Deker stripped and stuffed everything into the satchel Caleb had kindly provided, as well as two bronze daggers in case things got up close and personal on the other side of the river. Elezar followed suit, and they stepped down the limestone bank. They were joined by a gazelle that had ventured down to the watering hole.

The water was colder than Deker expected, the current stiffer. At any moment he felt he'd be swept off his feet. Deker had never seen the Jordan move so fast. He knew it dropped an average of three meters per kilometer until it emptied into the Dead Sea. But in the twenty-first century, most of that water had been siphoned off by agriculture.

He was getting a bad feeling about this.

He looked back, but Salmon and Achan and everything on the east bank of the river had disappeared behind the mist. Now he and Elezar had to wade through the void on their own to the unseen other side. It felt less like a flight to freedom than an Israeli-Palestinian prisoner exchange: there was always the outside chance you'd get shot in the back—or the front—before reaching the other side.

He could still feel the pain in his own back from the bronze spearhead that first brought him here, and he suddenly wondered what the wound looked like. Had they sewn him up back in Shittim? Would there be a scar, should he return to his own time? His mind went to a million places as his feet began to touch the bottom near the shallower middle of the river.

And then all of a sudden the current picked up, lifting him off his feet and sweeping him downstream. He started kicking and worked his legs furiously, treating the river like a riptide, swimming toward the western bank, afraid that if he stopped for even a moment he would sink to the bottom and never surface again.

Swallowing some water and choking all the way in, he crawled up on the west bank of the Jordan.

Elezar dragged himself up after him and said, "If the Lord doesn't part the waters, the Israelites will never make it."

"We made it. That's all that matters."

They ran up and over the bank, moving quickly through the

mist into a thick field of barley stalks. There they removed their clothing from their soaked satchels and dressed quickly. The rising sun would dry them soon enough.

Already the horizon was plain to see as the first light of day began to break. As Deker stuck his head above the stalks, he could see some baskets floating over the fields.

"The field workers have already started their day," Deker reported to Elezar, who was having trouble with his deerskin boots. "Let's pray to God they're good old Palestinians and this is the West Bank as we know it. Jericho is only four kilometers away. We can hit the Oasis Casino and grab lunch at The Mount of Temptation Restaurant before noon."

Deker and Elezar stood up and began to move through the golden stalks, passing curious workers and a few oxen along the way until they finally reached a wide, well-traveled dirt road.

"This isn't Route 90," Deker said quietly as he took in the still air. A sinking feeling of dread began to press down on him.

"That's because there *is* no Route 90, fool," Elezar told him. "There is *no West Bank*. There is *no Israel*. There is only *that*."

Deker followed Elezar's gaze to the northwest and started. Straight ahead in the distance, towering over an oasis of palm trees, were the grim walls of ancient Jericho, soaring darkly against the dawn.

Standing cold and damp, his legs still weak from the strength of the Jordan's current, Deker realized his hopes of walking into the arms of the modern-day, Israeli-occupied West Bank were shattered.

They had covered too much ground now, from the camp at

Shittim to the base at the Jordan and now across the Jordan, to hold on to the thin hope this was all some movie set. Nor could he pass off the megalithic structure on the horizon as some mirage or mental fabrication.

His presence in this ancient world—this time—was as unquestionable as those massive walls before him. And, as with time, there was nowhere to move but forward.

11

The well-worn road to Jericho was on a slight uphill grade, four kilometers beyond the west bank of the Jordan River. Deker was beginning to feel the exhaustion that should have overwhelmed him hours ago. His legs continued to ache even now from that grapevine hold the Israelites had put him into back at Shittim. The crossing of the Jordan hadn't helped. Bracing himself against the fast current had taken its toll on his already overtaxed muscles. His throat seemed to be perpetually parched in the dry air, and the unfamiliar scents of the field and vegetation on this side of the Jordan inflamed his sinuses, giving him a headache.

On second thought, he had had a headache ever since his torture back in Madaba.

Maybe it was the exhaustion or just the simple lack of plausible alternatives, but Deker had finally accepted Elezar's theory that they were now living among the ancients circa 1400 BC.

"If this is real, Elezar—if by some miracle or curse we're back in time—I refuse to live out the rest of my life hiding from history in hopes of not changing it. You said yourself, that horse has left the barn."

"Whatever fate has befallen us, we must see it through," Elezar said. "That means we follow the orders of our IDF superiors, and in this epoch that's General Bin-Nun. We spy out Jericho and get out before the gates close at sundown. Then we return to Shittim to give our report."

"And if we fail?"

"Then there might never be a Jewish nation, present or future. We're the Palestinians in this world, Deker, and the fortresses of Canaan might as well be modern Israel. Get used to it."

Elezar seemed a bit too eager to play a starring role in history by helping the Jews steamroll into the Promised Land. Deker, for his part, refused to surrender his own fate to history. But he had to wonder if the young zealot Salmon was right: this wasn't the plan. He and Elezar were not supposed to be here. If anything, their presence now could only threaten Israel's future, not ensure it.

And yet, where else could they run to in this world?

They were walking at a steady pace over the verdant land, passing early day laborers until the road widened as it bent toward Jericho and the hills beyond. Apart from the dust, they were dressed in the appropriate attire, and it amazed him that they looked as if they belonged in this land.

Field workers wore basic tunics while the traders and rich had finer clothing and jewelry: bronze cloak fasteners, gold bracelets and rings. The faces here didn't seem all that different from those he was familiar with across the Middle East, except that there were fewer beards than he expected, and mostly on older men like Elezar. Younger men shaved, the razor apparently having been invented some time ago.

The modern man in this world, much like himself, was a clean-shaven one.

Every now and then a convoy of oxen and carts carrying produce would pass by, the Bronze Age version of eighteen-wheelers. This was a trucking route as much as a passenger trade route. Deker and Elezar would acknowledge the drivers and workers with a nod but not exchange words.

The ground started to shake and for a moment Deker thought it was a seismic tremor. The region was riddled with faults. But when he looked back over his shoulder, he saw a cloud of dust coming their way as four horsemen thundered toward them.

"Must be military," Elezar said. "They'll be armed."

The patrol had to be based out of Jericho, Deker thought, as horses didn't have the long-distance water capacity of camels. They had probably made a circuit between the nearest highway oasis and the city.

Elezar said, "Move to the side of the road to let them pass."

But instead of speeding up, the horses began to slow down as they approached. Deker counted four armed soldiers dressed in the heavy body armor of the regular Reahn army—bronze helmets and breastplates—and radiating a distinctly menacing aura.

The nearer the horses came, the smaller Deker felt. He hadn't been next to a horse in years, and the pounding of the hooves on the packed dirt rattled his backbone. Their muscles rippled in their legs, their eyes blazed and foam formed around their mouths.

Deker would have gladly faced an armored tank instead of these fearsome, fast and powerful means of war.

"It's kill or be killed if we're blown," Elezar told him. "They go down or we do, and with us the future of Israel."

Deker couldn't argue with Elezar's first statement, or the rest. He instinctively reached back beneath his tunic and felt the bone handles of the two bronze daggers he had slipped behind his back.

12

The hoofbeats stopped as the patrol came to a halt just a few meters away from Deker and Elezar. The four Reahn soldiers were close enough for Deker to see the emblem of Jericho emblazoned on their breastplates: a six-pointed star exactly like the one on the flag of Israel.

"What's with the Star of David?" Deker whispered to Elezar.

"It's the Blazing Star of Remphan," Elezar told him. "Quick, pull out your IDF tag so they can see it."

Deker removed his hands from the dagger behind his back and made sure his dog tag was on full display over his tunic. "But it's Jewish."

"A six-pointed star could never be Jewish," Elezar chided him. "Six is the number of man. Seven, like our menorah, is the number of God. The Blazing Star is Egyptian in origin. It represents the star god Saturn or Molech."

"Molech?" Deker had heard the name back in Shittim.

"God of the Reahns and the name of the idol secretly worshiped by the Israelites in the wilderness. Moses had his Levites slay three thousand Israelites because of it. The six-pointed star was never a symbol of Judaism. It was Solomon, David's son, who made it a symbol of the state." Despite the circumstances, Elezar seemed to enjoy lecturing Deker on Jewish history once again.

Deker said nothing more as two of the soldiers dismounted and walked toward them, one wielding a scythe-like sword and the other carrying an axe. The commanding officer remained on his horse. The fourth Reahn, meanwhile, rose up in his stirrups, bow and arrow trained on them.

One of the stone-faced lieutenants barked in ancient Arabic, "Open your satchels for inspection."

Deker glanced at Elezar and understood that these thugs wanted a piece of whatever they might be carrying before they got to the main gate, which in itself suggested bribes and corruption were not tolerated within the city walls.

Deker wordlessly offered his satchel to the soldier, who ripped it open with his sword. Several pieces of jewelry fell to the ground.

"We are tradesmen," Elezar said as the sparkling gems in the dirt fixated the soldiers. "We were going to deposit these at the treasury in Reah."

"No you're not," said the commanding officer from his horse. "You're going to deposit them with us, and then I'll decide if I'm going to kill you and fertilize these fields with your flesh."

Deker watched the soldier closest to him bend over to pick up a piece of jewelry, revealing a full view of the bowman with his arrow ready to strike.

He glanced at Elezar, who seemed to be thinking the same

thing he was: *The whole mission will be shot to pieces before it even gets started.*

As the Reahn soldier bent over again, Deker saw his opportunity. He gave the soldier a knee to the face. The soldier snapped back upright, and Deker used him as a shield to take the arrow from the bowman. Then he grabbed the soldier's sword and hurled it at the bowman, catching him under the chin. The bowman grabbed at his throat and fell off his horse, dead.

The second dismounted soldier came at Deker, swinging his axe, ready to bring it down on Deker's head. Deker reached back and grabbed the two knives at the small of his back. Bringing both blades out in a flash, he plunged them into the soldier's gut, just beneath his breastplate. Blood gushed out as Deker withdrew the blades and the soldier fell forward dead.

He turned to Elezar, who had sliced the captain on his horse but failed to bring him down. Now the horse and its rider were taking off, and Deker couldn't have that.

Deker picked up the dead bowman's bow and arrow from the ground, drew back the string and aimed. The arrow wobbled through the air and overshot the horse. But his target was still within the one-hundred-meter range for one more shot. He picked up another arrow and pointed, aiming a few degrees higher for loft, and let go.

The arrow missed the rider but hit the horse, and down it went.

Deker ran with an axe in hand as the captain struggled to get out from under his mount. The man's leg was pinned painfully below the fallen horse. It took only a single blow to crush the captain's helmet and the skull beneath. Still the Reahn fought, striking out at Deker with his fist even as blood seeped out of his smashed helmet.

Deker brought up his axe to finish him off and felt a sharp pain as the Reahn thrust a dagger into his leg. Deker shouted and brought the axe down again on the captain's face, and the Reahn's limbs flopped to the ground, his thick fist opening up until the dagger fell from his lifeless fingers.

Deker's shout faded away over the field until there was only the whinnying of the wounded horse.

At the sound of the cracking of a stalk behind him, Deker spun around to see a bloodied Elezar pulling the two live horses he had captured. He was dressed in a Reahn uniform, which hung on his lean frame. Beneath the bronze breastplate he had on a red tunic, belted with leather and cinched up to keep the tunic from falling below his knees. His brown leather boots were part sandal, part shin guard. And the breastplate's six-pointed star shone brightly in the sun, as if the body armor's owner had polished it daily. But the bronze helmet was tipped too far back on his head, and Elezar had missed the smudge of blood on his chin strap.

"Change of plans," Elezar said, and stopped suddenly as he took in what was left of Deker's theater of war.

Deker stood there motionless, his fist loosening just enough to let his Reahn battle-axe hit the ground with a thud.

Elezar stared down at the dead rider and dying horse with a look of horror and fascination. Deker watched his superior officer's eyes drift up his blood-soaked body until they locked on his own.

"Maybe I was wrong about you, Deker. You might make a good Jew yet."

13

Dazed, Deker gazed at the blood all over himself, human and horse. The cold-blooded brutality of such close combat was very different from the relatively detached, remote-control work of bombs and the instant disintegration of body parts they caused. He had seen the results of his handiwork before, but rarely inflicted death with his own bloody hands.

Deker hated death almost as much as himself for his efficiency at dispensing it. That his own life was at stake, and even the future of his people, did little to lessen his guilt and self-loathing.

Now, as he took in his handiwork, the old nausea was coming back as it had at the scene of Rachel's death. Several had been killed in that blast, and he had refused to look. But he had seen a mangled limb fried to a cinder, and while he had told himself it wasn't Rachel's, it could have been, and he could not sleep for almost two months afterward.

"Deker!" Elezar spoke, bringing him out of his daze. "Clean yourself up."

Elezar tossed him a dirty tunic to use as a rag.

"You're a bloody mess," Elezar told him. "Your cover garb is of no use to us now. You're going to have to piece together a uniform from the body parts you've scattered around here. We'll go in as soldiers and use their papers to get through the gate."

As Deker mopped up blood, a muffled roar of pain came from deep within the dying horse. To Deker's amazement, the horse valiantly struggled back on its feet.

"Step back," he told Elezar.

Wiping the blood from his eyes, Deker swore and took his blade, plunging it into the horse's side to put them both out of their misery. The horse collapsed and disappeared beneath the tops of the stalks. The shimmering field of grain was calm and peaceful again, as if horses and riders had never been.

But it wouldn't hide the carnage for long, Deker thought as he looked at the broken grain stalks around him, covered with blood. Already a lone raven circled overhead like some Predator drone. Soon there would be more crows. A black cloud would hover over the fields like a column of dark smoke rising into the air, a beacon to any and all atop Jericho's watchtowers.

"We're losing time, Deker," Elezar said impatiently.

Deker looked at the noonday sun. Elezar was right. They'd be lucky to get in before the gates closed at sunset. Luckier still to make it out before the Reahns knew one of their patrols hadn't reported back and was missing. Before long the hunt would be on for them. They had to clean up and get out before anybody spotted them.

Unfortunately, somebody already had.

Behind Elezar, Deker saw a small face in the stalks, eyes wide open. It was a boy, no older than ten, staring at the bloody clothes on the ground and the dead horse and soldier.

Before Deker could speak, Elezar's hand plunged into the stalks and pulled out the screaming boy by the hair before he quickly shut him up with a hand over his mouth and a blade to his throat.

"No!" Deker told Elezar, watching the boy squirm in Elezar's arms. "He's just a boy, a kid who works in the fields."

Elezar began to press the blade into the small, tender throat, and the boy's wild eyes grew even wider. "He has a mouth, doesn't he? If we let him go, we might as well blow the warning horns from the towers of Jericho ourselves."

"He's a boy, Elezar."

"Yes, and in our time he'd probably be strapped with explosives, and we'd already be dead."

"But this isn't our time."

"It is now, Deker, and you know it."

Deker paused and took a breath. With each passing second the sun was moving faster and the shadows of the walls were growing longer. "We tie and gag him," he finally said. "The end is the same: we've kept him quiet long enough for us to get inside the city before the gates close."

Elezar squinted at him in what Deker could only interpret as profound disappointment and even disgust. "I take back what I said just now about you being a good Jew," he said, putting his blade away and instead tightening his bare hands around the boy's neck in a chokehold. The boy struggled to breathe. "But I need you for this mission."

Elezar's hands squeezed hard until they crushed the boy's windpipe and he collapsed to the ground. Deker ran to the prostrate child and bent over the pale, bluish face struggling for air. The boy had a pulse but looked like he didn't know it.

"You're a heartless son of a bitch, Elezar."

"He'll live to see tomorrow, Deker. Which is more than I can say for you and me unless we move our asses."

14

Jericho. City of the Moon. Reah, as the Reahns who worshiped the celestial and lunar deities called it. The city looked like a piece of the moon had crashed to earth in the middle of a tropical oasis. Its walls seemed to rise more than fifty meters above the surrounding palm trees. The late-afternoon sun only lengthened the walls' ominous shadows—and shortened the time Deker and Elezar had to make it to the main gate before it closed at dusk.

They rode side by side along the wide entrance road, dressed in the uniforms of the Reahn soldiers they had killed and buried back in the fields. They had passed a couple of chariots and a number of oxen pulling empty carts. The farmers had already brought their goods to market and were returning. Now the traffic was heavier flowing out of the city than in. That would only draw more attention to them when they tried to enter the city gate.

More fortress than city, Jericho's profile resembled a giant aircraft carrier cut from a single rock. All the fortifications were aimed at the single main gate in its narrow eastern wall at the bow, pointed like the barrel of a giant cannon at any who approached her.

The monolithic walls began to separate into two as the road bent to reveal the main gate. Deker could see that there were really two walls around the city.

The lower outer wall ringed the base of the city mound. It boasted an impressive five-meter-high concrete revetment skirt at the base. The rest of the outer wall, comprising red bricks, rose another ten meters to the parapets on top, where uniformed soldiers with gleaming spears marched between two stone watchtowers on the north and south walls.

The city's higher inner wall ringed the fortress at its summit. This wall was almost fifteen meters high and also built of red bricks, with two additional stone towers on its east and west walls. All the towers had slits for the archers. They might as well be housing machine guns, Derek thought, because either way the targets of their fire would be shredded to death in seconds.

Jericho's layers of defense at first glance were proving to be far more impressive than Deker had anticipated. So shocked was Deker at this level of engineering that he once again doubted if he was in fact in ancient times or dreaming all this up. The challenge taking shape both perturbed him and yet strangely excited him.

Soaring high above the city's walls and the four watchtowers was Jericho's landmark octagonal spire. It resembled a giant Muslim minaret with a watchtower on top, and afforded the Reahn army 360-degree visibility of all lines of approach. From that vantage, Deker didn't doubt the Reahns could see the pillar of smoke from the Israelite camp at Shittim.

He also doubted that anybody up there could miss him and Elezar as they rode up to the wide stone ramp leading to Jericho's massive and iconic iron gate.

An iron gate in the Bronze Age, Deker thought. There was no greater symbol of strength and impregnability in this world.

Deker took in the red banners with the black six-pointed Blazing Star on a circular white field draped from the walls. It was the same color scheme the Nazis used to unfurl their swastikas. He also noted the sun sinking rapidly behind the dark ridge of hills to the north. By now the ravens must have led to the discovery of the slain patrol. All it would take was a smoke signal or blast of a horn in the distance to alert the gate.

"Even if we beat the gate, we're going to lose the light," he warned Elezar.

"Just stick to inspection of the fortifications, Deker, and let me do the talking," Elezar shot back quietly. "Maybe, just maybe, we'll live to see tomorrow."

They dismounted and walked their horses up to a line of three camels and a cart at the gate's entrance. Two armored chariots flanked the gate while Reahn soldiers with scythe blades and spears inspected every sack and person entering the fortress city. More soldiers on the ramparts of the wall paced back and forth, their eyes fixed on the line below. Beyond them was a second line of archers and slingers in the east tower of the fortress above. Deker could pick out their shadows moving behind the slits in the stone.

The gatehouse was a garrison unto itself, with two dozen Reahn guards and passport inspectors checking papers, baskets and weapons. Two gigantic bronze doors ten meters high, now open, guarded the gatehouse tunnel through the five-meter-thick city wall. The tunnel itself was rife with murder holes for Reahn archers and spearmen to cut down anybody who managed to slip through the heavy doors as they closed. But that seemed unlikely to Deker. For hanging overhead in front of the massive doors was a heavy portcullis made of crossed iron bars, ready to drop like a guillotine should the city come under attack.

A military official waved them up to the gate and Elezar handed over their military papers, stamped with the seal of General Hamas himself. An orderly, meanwhile, led their horses to a stable door inside the southern wall of the gatehouse tunnel. That told Deker some sections of the wall were hollowed out for storage of food and other supplies. Depending on the nature of the fill, some sections of the outer wall were either less stable or more reinforced than others.

The Reahn official then looked about for the rest of the patrol and frowned. "Where are the rest?"

"Back at the last oasis checkpoint, detaining foreigners," Elezar said. "They'll be here soon enough. This couldn't wait."

Elezar unfurled the leather wrap with the jewelry, and Deker gauged the official's attention.

The official seemed surprised by nothing, as he had probably seen everything in this post. Nor did he display even a hint of temptation to help himself to any bribe. The ranks of Reahns were apparently more loyal to Hamas—or afraid of him—than Bin-Nun believed.

"This isn't the protocol," the agent said.

"This isn't your business," Elezar said sharply, using his natural arrogance to full effect. "But then, you can explain our delay to Hamas yourself."

The agent paused, a pained expression creeping across his stone face. "Carry on," he said, and they were cleared to enter Jericho.

15

As soon as they cleared the gate, Deker and Elezar found themselves in Jericho's main market square. The square was a flat acre in size and nestled between the main gate and the upper fortress wall. It was a deceptively cheerful, noisy scene, with splashes of color from the shop awnings, fabrics and ceramics. But the troops patrolling the ramparts on both walls above gave Deker the distinct impression that the prosperous ancients shopping and trading in the square below were, in the end, nothing but better-dressed rats in a stone cage.

"It won't be long before they figure out what happened to the patrol," Elezar whispered as they walked. "You're going to have to make your assessments quickly if we're to have any hope of getting out before the gate closes."

Deker nodded. Like everything else in this world, Jericho paradoxically struck him as smaller than he had envisioned and yet more formidable just the same. Jericho's mound looked to be barely eight acres if that, maybe the size of six square blocks in modern midtown Manhattan.

"I've got the pop count here at three thousand—maybe four thousand during the day when it swells from workers and tradesmen from the surrounding areas," Deker said, applying the ancient numerical ratio of five hundred people per urban acre. "That gives us a troop count of anywhere between eight hundred to fifteen hundred tops."

Elezar must have detected the dismay in his voice, because he asked, "Meaning what, exactly?"

"Meaning who needs Yahweh when you outnumber the Reahns ten to one?" Deker replied.

"Maybe Bin-Nun should even the odds by instead attacking Hazor to the north with its population of thirty thousand," Elezar said in an icy monotone. "You forget we're but two men in this city of three thousand. That's fifteen-hundred-to-one. You like those odds? And what about the mysterious 'shadow army' that Caleb and Bin-Nun are so worried about? Their ranks, if they exist, could number like the stars in the heavens or the grains of sand in the sea."

Deker said nothing and looked up at the sheer fortress wall that rose above them like a stone monolith with nothing but a horizontal slit near the top for still more faceless slingers and archers. Beyond it, the city's signature spire tower rose higher still. Even if the Israelites could ladder over the city wall in superior numbers, they'd be blocked by this even more immense wall inside, surrounded by the spearmen and soldiers on the ramparts above.

"Ladders are no good," Deker reported. "The first five meters of that concrete revetment wall will kill them before they even reach the rest of the city wall. All the while, the archers on the ramparts have clear shots from every angle. Then there are the four main towers, two along the lower city walls and two more along the upper fortress walls. On top of that, there's the fifth tower rising above the entire city."

They could barely see the glint of spears moving back and forth on the ramparts as they walked. Above them was the second line of sharpshooters atop the fortress wall and, above them all, the stone spire.

Tunneling was out too, Deker could see. The city wall extended belowground, thanks to its concrete skirt, and the city itself sat on a mound inside. As for a sneak attack through the sewer system, the drainage holes were too small for a man to crawl through, and the main well for freshwater, just to their south, had to drop fifteen meters to the natural spring below. It was guarded with its own platoon of Reahn troops and topped with iron crossbars like the main gate. A huge circular stone the size of one of those monster dolmen slabs back at Shittim sat nearby, and Deker expected the Reahns used it to seal off the well any time they closed the main gate.

"You look and I'll listen," Elezar said.

They joined the foot traffic moving between the market district and the commercial district on the city's south side. Deker noted the large number of metalworkers, carpenters and masons. They would be the ones who reinforced the walls whenever earth tremors or water damage eroded their foundations. Then there were the tanners, potters, tailors, bakers and cheese makers he would have expected. One small winery employed workers to stomp on grapes. Their hands had been cut off. Theft was no more tolerated here than bribes.

Most striking to Deker was the grain. It was everywhere: over-flowing from jars, drying in stalks on rooftops, being carried back and forth in baskets. This was the harvest in the land of milk and honey. The people were shoving grain into every silo and orifice in the city. And the flow of a water chute from the fortress above suggested massive water cisterns of the kind found on the Temple Mount in Jerusalem.

"Everything looks fine, but I smell fear," Deker said. "They're pretending like there's no threat of an invasion. But they're pre-paring for one just the same."

"That's good," Elezar said.

"No, that's bad. Because they have enough grain and water to outlast an Israelite siege for years."

The reality was that, at first glance, Deker didn't see how Bin-Nun could avoid taking Jericho without suffering massive casual-ties. The losses in such a so-called victory would break the back of his war machine, demoralize the Israelites and open them to attack by Jericho's stronger neighbors in Canaan.

The walls had to come down first, somehow. There simply was no other way. And yet, the longer their shadows grew from the setting sun, the taller and more impregnable those walls appeared.

Elezar seemed to read his mind. "So, could you bring down the walls with your C-4?"

"I thought that was Yahweh's job."

"Maybe we are God's hand."

Deker asked, "How did the walls come down in Scripture?"

"The book of Joshua says the walls fell outward, not inward, and the Israelites marched single file up into the city."

Deker nodded as he looked around. The trick was ultimately going to be to find a compromised or hollow part of the upper wall and plant the C-4. That would steer the rest of the wall in the proper direction as it collapsed. If he did it right, he could actually use the avalanche set off by the wall cascading down the sloping city to take out a portion of the lower wall to boot. And if he was truly brilliant, the resulting collapse of the city wall would create its own ramp over that lower concrete wall at the bottom.

"It's possible," Deker said. "In theory, it's no different than dropping a high-rise in Tel Aviv. But it's still a huge job and requires careful planning. We need to get a look inside that upper fortress."

They began searching for a second gate that connected the upper fortress with the lower city, and found what they were looking for at the end of the commercial district: a guarded bronze gate in the upper wall. The gate was open to reveal wide stone steps leading up to the fortress, where a massive temple, fountains, royal courtyard and government buildings could be glimpsed.

But as they stepped toward the bronze gate, the blast of a horn sounded from a watchtower and a colored flag went up the stone spire. A platoon of shock troops emerged from the fortress and headed straight toward them.

Leading the way was the little boy whom Deker had spared, his throat wrapped with some kind of bandage. He also had a black eye now, swollen shut. He was on some sort of leash, like an ancient bloodhound. His open and animated eye darted to and fro, looking for them, as if his life depended on it even more than when Elezar had held a blade to his throat.

"They found the patrol," Elezar said. "They know we're here. We're blown."

Deker turned away from Elezar's accusing eyes as they beat a hasty retreat through the thinning crowds of the market square at dusk. They arrived just in time to see the main gate close with the clanking of chains and an earthshaking thud, sealing them inside.

16

Standing in the middle of the market square, Deker quickly saw they were blocked on three sides: by the advancing police troops from the city's south side, the wall of the fortress to their west, and the closed city gate to their east. That left them only one direction of escape.

"Rahab's Inn," Deker said. "It must be on the other side of the square."

He heard no argument from the purse-lipped Elezar as they disappeared into the twisting alleys of the city's cramped north side. This part of town was further stratified, with the better housing uphill against the outside of the fortress wall above them and the slums pressed against the inside of the lower city wall.

They hurried onto one of two main boulevards lined with palm trees that swayed in the darkening sky, then turned into an alley, emerging in another square. The evening was alive with small groups of Reahns strolling about and filling up the taverns. If there was a nightly curfew, it was still a few hours away, and the inhabitants of the city had long ago made their peace with the presence of troops and police searches in their lives.

"This is it," Deker said, pointing to the red scarves hanging from the windows of the brothels around the square. "The red-light district. Wasn't Rahab the hooker supposedly spared when Jericho fell because she tied a scarlet cord in her window so that the Israelite troops would avoid her house?"

"Figures she's the only thing you'd remember from Hebrew school," Elezar quipped as he scanned the surroundings.

"Not that it helps us," Deker said. "Almost every window here has a red scarf."

It was a shabby but busy area dotted with fruit stands, sweet-shops and taverns that encircled the square. Elezar made a bee-line for an outside table stacked high with dates and pomegran-ates on one side and jars and cups on the other. The old Reahn woman behind the table didn't even wait to pour them two cups of pomegranate juice.

Deker downed the sweet juice in one giant gulp. He realized he hadn't eaten all day, not since the night before in Shittim.

Elezar played it better, taking a sip and nodding his appre-ciation before he placed the cup down, wiped his mouth with his hand and simply asked, "Rahab?"

The woman seemed puzzled that any man would have to ask, but her eyes drifted to the four-story villa above a tavern and opposite what appeared to be the local police station. It was an open-fronted building with a courtyard on the square filled with straw chairs arranged under the trees.

And packed under those trees, drinking the local ale, smoking the local weeds and playing a game with small pegs while they waited to be serviced, were a dozen Reahn officers.

"We're fucked," Deker said under his breath.

"For both our sakes, I hope you're right, Deker," Elezar replied. "Reahn custom prevents these men from barging into a woman's room. They must ask permission to enter. Let's go," he said, and started for the inn.

17

Deker saw a lot of strange faces and could hear a number of different languages around the tavern as he and Elezar made their way through a large crowd of drunken Reahn soldiers and the bar wenches who served them. At the counter in back, the inn manager, a slight, dark man, looked visibly irked at being pulled aside on a busy night.

"We're looking for Rahab," Elezar said.

"You and everybody else," the manager said, looking them over. "You don't have the rank."

"Maybe this does," Deker said, and removed from his neck the necklace with the crescent-shaped pendant that Caleb had given them and handed it to the manager.

The manager frowned and looked up at him curiously. "Two specials for our guests," he called to one of his bar wenches. He then disappeared into a back hallway while a young girl served them a couple of locally brewed drinks.

Deker looked out over the tables to the plaza beyond, watching for trouble. Elezar's ears, meanwhile, were up like antennae as they sipped their drinks. The brew tasted like a cross between beer and ouzo.

"They're all talking about Bin-Nun," Elezar whispered. "The Israelites are undefeated in war and marching to Canaan. The bets are that he'll hit Jericho first once the Jordan is past flood stage in a month or two. Then they'll swarm Canaan like cockroaches. If only all the cities united with a national army, it would be the end of the vermin. If anyone can stop them, it's Hamas. He's got a secret army to defeat even Yahweh."

"What is it?" Deker asked.

"Nobody knows. But some are worried Hamas is talking about doubling Reah's offerings to Molech."

Before Deker could ask what that meant, the inn manager returned and said, "We've got rooms and girls for you both."

"I'm not interested in your girls," Elezar scoffed.

"Then I've got boys for you."

Elezar's face turned red. "That won't be necessary. I only want a room for the night and privacy."

"You, old and ugly, follow me," the manager told Elezar, and then looked at Deker. "You, young and handsome, follow her. She'll take you to Rahab."

The manager was pointing to a young girl no older than thirteen—a belly dancer, by the looks of her satin top, flowing pants, bells and glitter, and not a professional yet.

As Deker followed the girl down a long hallway, he began to

wonder what he would actually have to do with this woman Rahab in order to secure her help in escaping capture. Elezar had suggested she was likely two decades Deker's senior, and old Caleb had warned from the outset that she was not to be trusted and should be treated only as their last resort. Apparently there was no such thing as a hooker with a heart of gold in this world, only a hooker with a heart *for* gold.

Deker and the girl emerged into a cobbled courtyard surrounded by walls. One of those walls was the city wall itself, rising up five meters before his eyes. He could see a Reahn helmet and spear floating at the top.

There was a gate at the far end of the courtyard and, on the right, stone steps leading to the upper levels of the villa, a level higher than even the city wall. This was where the girl stopped and allowed him to continue alone.

As Deker climbed from one level to the next, a magnificent view unfolded below him. There were the catwalks and guards on the walls, and beyond the city he could see the dark hills to the north rolling beneath the moon.

At the top of the steps he emerged onto a broad terrace. There was the scent of almond trees as he passed through an iron gate into a semitropical paradise. The sound of water was everywhere, splashing in fountains and gurgling in the conduits as it dropped from terrace to terrace between palm trees.

In the center was a large divan with a rainbow of colorful pillows. To the side was a long table of jars and bowls of fruit beneath a pergola. The pergola had golden flax stalks piled on top, no doubt to dry during the day, which lent a Polynesian air to the terrace.

Deker watched the door in the wall on the opposite side, waiting for Rahab to appear. But the door remained shut, and he walked over to the table beneath the pergola and helped himself to some dates. There he noticed one of the ornamental bowls was filled to the top with gold coins.

Only then was he aware that she was already there. He put the dates down and turned to see her. She was standing at the balustrade of the terrace, looking out across the desert at the pillar of fire in the distance: the signal tower at Shittim.

Her silhouette against the stars was a thing of beauty, and as his eyes adjusted to the nighttime, he could see her black mane of hair dropping between her bare shoulder blades.

Elezar was wrong. This is a young woman.

She was in some kind of silk wrap that rippled in the breeze, the moonlight revealing a flawless figure underneath. And when she turned to face him, he caught his breath.

Rachel.

The high cheekbones, the wide-set and intelligent eyes and the birthmark over her soft upper lip he could never forget. She could be nobody other than Rachel. Even the way her lustrous hair framed her perfect face was exactly the way he remembered her.

Deker could feel her smoky gaze study him as she floated toward him, charging the air around her with palpable electricity. Then she unclipped the bronze clasp on her wrap, and he watched the silk fall like feathers to the tiles to reveal herself to him.

She was wearing the necklace he had brought. The pendant dangled between her full breasts, round as the moon in the sky.

"I've been waiting for you," she told him in Hebrew. Her voice was soft but confident.

"Waiting for me?" he asked, astonished. "How long?"

"My whole life," she said, and then she kissed him with the most delicious lips he had ever tasted.

18

Deker stood there slack-jawed before this girl. And she was just a girl, perhaps only seventeen or eighteen, which was Rachel's age as he remembered her. But even Rachel hadn't been this beautiful, and that alone bothered Deker. He began to wonder what sort of fantasy he now held in his arms. Everything inside him told him to run, but her lips felt warm to his as she kissed him again and placed his hands on her breasts. He dared not let go, afraid she might vanish before his eyes.

She smiled as she lifted one of his hands and used it to lead him to her bed—the king-size divan strewn with pillows of assorted shapes and sizes. And without a further word they began to make love to each other under the stars, as if it were the most natural thing in the universe and they had known each other forever.

Her body moved with a grace and in a way that suggested she had all the time in the world. His body responded in a way that suggested he would accept nothing short of eternity with her. She was bringing him to life, and he suddenly felt more awake than he had in years. He could feel his heart beating again, the blood coursing through his veins and pure electricity tingling across his entire body.

Somewhere deep inside, the hard shell around his soul began to crack, light bursting through. The passion for life he had once shared with Rachel, the spontaneity he thought he would never feel again—that force of nature rose up inside him with a volcanic power that couldn't be contained. He felt his spirit burst free into pure ecstatic flight.

Only when it was over and they were back in each other's arms on her divan beneath the starry sky, her long, soft legs draped over his own, did he realize that Rahab was not, in fact, his Rachel.

Rahab was taller than Rachel, her raven hair a lighter chestnut color instead of the black he had first imagined. And, yes, more beautiful still. That this was what he should first notice deeply tormented him, and he looked into her eyes, bottomless black pools in which any man could easily drown.

"You said you were waiting for me your whole life. What did you mean?" he finally asked her.

She looked at him curiously, and he realized that while she understood what he said, his accent had thrown her. It was clearly strange and exotic to her ears. He watched her fingers slide down the chain around her neck to the crescent moon lying on her right breast.

"My grandmother, Rahab, gave this necklace to General Bin-Nun forty years ago when he spied out the land and stayed at our family's inn," she told him. "He wasn't a general then, but young and handsome like you. And cut like you."

He realized she was talking about his circumcision. "And your family inn?"

"Just an inn at the time," she said. "Bin-Nun assured my grandmother that Moses and the Israelites were coming. She died still waiting. But she lived long enough to see the former Egyptian colonies in Canaan grow more tyrannical, our inn turn into a fertility temple and my mother forced into becoming a priestess. She was only a few years older than I am now when the priests of Molech told her she was getting too old to bless the land. They started me when I was eleven. I built the business, brought in the foreign traders, cut the deals with the priests and the king. Now I run all the girls here—and the officers of Reah too."

There was some pride in her voice, and Deker could only imagine the course she had had to navigate to achieve her pinnacle of power and influence.

"Yet, you clung to your belief that one day another young Hebrew spy might show up at your doorstep?"

"News of Bin-Nun's victories in Moab in recent months and the fear gripping Reah told me as much. Your presence in my bed tells me that the attack is coming any day now. And my informants tell me Hamas has his men doing a house-to-house search for you and your comrade at this very moment."

Suddenly he felt extremely vulnerable, naked with this woman who held his life in the palm of her hand. Any second she could turn him over to Hamas or the troops searching for him throughout the city.

"You know my name," she asked him. "What's yours?"

"Samuel."

"Son of?"

"My full name is Samuel Boaz Deker," he told her, dispensing with pseudonyms or code names, since his name meant nothing in this world.

She began to nod slowly. "That is very . . . Hebrew."

It was, and he had resented it as a child, sticking to "Sam Deker" to anyone who asked. "That's what I am. A Jew."

It was the first time in his life that he had said it out loud to anybody, including himself. He had never hidden it nor been ashamed of his ethnic identity. He had certainly been reminded he was a Jew often enough by his nana with her Auschwitz tattoo, his parents and his peers in L.A. But he had never fully allowed himself to be defined by such an identity. He was always something else too. A Jewish American. A secular Jew. A Jew who didn't look like a Jew, sound like a Jew or date many Jews. Never just "a Jew."

Yet, in this world, that's exactly what he was and all that mattered to anybody that mattered: the Hebrews in Shittim and the Reahns in Jericho.

Samuel Boaz Deker.

Jew.

"I see sadness around your eyes when you look at me, Samuel Boaz Deker," she said. "I remind you of someone you lost."

"Yes."

"How did you lose her?"

"I killed her."

"Oh."

She looked at him curiously but without judgment.

"It was an accident," he told her quietly. "There was a bowl, like the one you keep your coins in on that table."

She glanced at the money bowl and then back at him, confused. "I think I misunderstand you."

He said nothing.

"I have lost those I love too." She was fingering his IDF dog tag. "My sisters. But it was no accident."

"Surely it couldn't have been your fault, either."

He could feel her body tremble slightly in his arms. The scent of her hair smelled like pomegranates. For whatever reason, she was as racked with guilt over her sisters as he was over Rachel. Neither he nor she fully understood each other's guilt. But Deker sensed they shared its depth, each in their own way, and so were linked together intimately and forever.

Rahab knew it too.

She began to trace the points of his Blazing Star with her finger, naming the six stars they represented: "Regulus, Altair, Eridani, Sirius, Arcturus, Ceti."

Deker rolled onto his back and looked up at the pergola. It was a square against the stars. He realized this was what she had seen every night, probably since she was eleven. The six stars formed a map of the heavens for the prophets.

"See the constellation of the Hippopotamus?" she asked him, and pointed up to what he recognized as the Big Dipper. "She is the goddess of creation. Tell me what you see inside her womb."

He saw a bright star, Mizar. But next to it was the far fainter Alcor, barely visible to the naked eye. They were known as the Horse and Rider, and he knew that the ancient Romans in several centuries—and IDF millennia later—would test the eyesight of their troops by their ability to detect the two as separate stars.

"I see twins," he told her. "You call them Israel and Ishmael?"

She smiled. "Half the archers see only the bigger star. Hamas puts them on spear duty on the lower north wall. The true marksmen he puts in the towers of the upper fortress wall. Our allies to the north and south think they have a range of three hundred cubits beyond the city wall. But Hamas has altered their bows and trained the archers to extend their range to almost five hundred cubits. Best if the Israelites keep that distance when they first surround our city."

Deker peered into her eyes. "Why are you divulging this information to me?"

"Because the stars proclaim the birth of the king of Israel," she told him. "The king of Reah and all his priests know it, and this is why they are desperate to stop you no matter what the cost."

Deker remembered Caleb's instruction to gauge the morale of the Reahns. He resented that intrusion into this moment, but her question compelled his own.

"So the people are scared?"

"Ever since they heard how your god Yahweh dried up the Red Sea for you when you came out of Egypt forty years ago," she told him. "But it's what you did to Sihon and Og, the two kings whom you utterly destroyed on the other side of the Jordan, that moved the noblemen to action. They sacked the previous commander of the army and brought in Hamas. Then they began a program to reinforce the fortifications and stockpile supplies in case of a long siege."

"What about you?" Deker asked her, thinking of Phineas sharpening the end of his spear back at Shittim even now. "Aren't you scared?"

"Of you, Samuel Boaz Deker, no," she said. "But I know that the Lord your God is God, in heaven above and on earth below, and He has given the Hebrews this land He originally promised us. Your army will kill us all. Every man, woman and child. Even our animals. Every breathing thing."

"You don't seem surprised."

"Yahweh is angry with us. We have abandoned him."

"You believe in Yahweh?"

"Abraham was my forefather, too, when God promised him this land," she told him.

"Don't you think Yahweh is cruel for instructing Bin-Nun to utterly destroy Reah and all the inhabitants of Canaan?"

She looked at him as if he were insane. "Perhaps it is I who have mistaken you for someone else," she said. "While our Hebrew cousins were slaves in Egypt for four hundred years, we Reahns and all the Amorites around us only increased in our wickedness from generation to generation. Even Pharaoh let your people go. But Hamas won't let us out of Reah, choosing instead to use our people as a shield."

Deker was intrigued by the use of human shields this early in warfare and listened to learn if this was perhaps the shadow army Bin-Nun feared. Perhaps that was why he pursued his take-no-prisoners, death-to-all strategy. But from what Rahab was saying, the Reahns cared less for their own people's lives than the Israelites did.

"What of your family?"

"I have no sisters, only brothers," she explained. "My sisters were burnt alive as offerings to Molech. I was spared only to serve Molech as a priestess, because my mother could not bear to lose another girl. And the girls who work for me and get pregnant must carry their babies to live births, even if it costs them their lives, because a priestess can have no scars. The babies we bury alive or throw screaming into the fires of the temple. Even the land, the lushest in the desert, is becoming polluted from our sins as a people and will not see another harvest like this one."

There was silence as Deker pondered her words. Then he heard the scraping of boots and voices from inside the villa.

Rahab stood up and put on her wrap. A servant girl came in and spoke to Rahab quickly while Deker buckled up his uniform.

He couldn't hear the conversation but knew the answer even before Rahab turned and told him.

"It's Hamas," she said. "They're here."

19

A minute later the hulking figure of Hamas walked onto the terrace. Deker couldn't see his face from his position atop the pergola, where he lay facedown between two blankets of flax stalks. But Hamas had taken off his helmet out of respect for Rahab, and through a slit Deker was able to look down and see the long mane of black hair falling over the Reahn general's broad shoulders. Hamas looked just over six feet tall, with a powerful trunk and legs that moved under the bronze plates and leather joints of his body armor.

A gruff voice in ancient Aramaic said, "You serviced two strangers tonight."

"The king's cut is in the bowl," Rahab replied.

She was dressed again in her wrap and seated on her divan, and Deker now saw that the surrounding tiles of the terrace formed a great mosaic of a six-pointed star that mirrored the heavens. And in the center of that blazing star was Rahab's bed.

"That's not why I'm here," Hamas said as he nonetheless

walked over to the red-and-black ceramic bowl of coins just below the pergola. It sat next to a small, bronze jewelry box. Deker watched Hamas remove a small money pouch from his belt and fill it with coins from the bowl. "Your girls serviced two Israelite spies tonight. Show me their rooms and I'll make it quick."

"I can tell a Hebrew from a Reahn? You'll have to round up everybody in the house. Then everybody will know you let two spies into the city."

Hamas paused in a way that suggested he knew what Rahab was up to and didn't like it. "The Jordan is at flood stage. Even if Bin-Nun could get his armies across, it would take three days. The king has no fear of imminent attack nor of these spies."

"Why are you here, then?"

"It's the traitors inside these walls that concern us more than the Israelites outside."

Hamas poured himself a drink from a pitcher at the table. He lifted the bronze cup to his lips and downed it in one long gulp. He poured himself another.

"Our people who fear the cult of Yahweh are fools. Plagues on Egypt. Parted seas. All lies. My family lived in Egypt at the time. I was five when it happened, Rahab. The waves, the hail, the pestilence and even the gases that killed our firstborn sons who slept on the floor, as was our custom—all were natural consequences of the volcanic eruption of Thera in the Great Sea.

"Bin-Nun knows this. He knows he can't repeat these wonders. He can't even feed his people without raids on farmlands and disrupting trade routes. He can't occupy a city, so he has to slaughter every breathing thing in it and call it a miracle. This cult of death is Bin-Nun's only weapon, and he employs it now to weaken the will of our people.

"He knows if he breaks our will—our true wall—our stones will crumble too. And then where would you be, Rahab? Slaughtered like every other man, woman and child in Reah."

Hamas downed the second drink, slammed the cup down and wiped his long sleeve across his mouth.

"You can never trust a Jew. But you can always trust me to do what I say I'll do. And you know what I do to the families of traitors. You saw what I had to do to your grandparents."

Well, there was the leverage, Deker thought. Not a scratch on Rahab. But death to those close to her. Her soul and his were more similar than he realized, as she had clearly carried the guilt for the loss of her sisters and felt responsible for the safety of the rest of her family.

"Then you're no better than Bin-Nun."

"Oh, I'm a lot better for *you*. Look at you, at what you have. You're the richest woman in Reah. You're a goddess. We worship you like Molech. Your body cycles with the moon and the crops. You are the heart of our city, not that."

Deker could see that Hamas was gesturing to her bed in the center of the blazing star painted on the terrace tiles.

"Bin-Nun would cut you down like he did those Moabite women who fornicated with his precious Hebrew soldiers," Hamas went on, going in for the kill. "A blade through that soft tummy of yours, after he cut off your breasts. The Jews can barely keep a dozen of their divine 613 laws. You think they'd let you—a whore who has broken them all—into their company and pull them down?"

The psychology was brilliant, and Deker could see Rahab cast a glance up at him, her eyes doubtful.

"I, on the other hand, appreciate your many hidden talents," Hamas said, and began to loosen his belt. "Your comely womanhood blesses our crops in tandem with your cycles of fertility. And your dexterous tongue loosens those of visiting dignitaries, providing us with invaluable information and even state secrets. All this while you pass along to them the false information we give you. Now, unless I hear something interesting from your mouth, I have a better use for it."

Hamas turned his back to the pergola, dropped to his knees and straddled Rahab with his blackened and bulging quadriceps, hamstrings and calves. Then he ripped off her wrap to behold her breasts like the ripest fruit in Reah.

Deker couldn't stomach the sight of her about to be ravaged, even if she meant to distract Hamas. Slowly he slid the tip of his sword through a slit in the flax stalks, ready to use both hands to drive the blade down on top of Hamas' head.

"If you want to perform your religious duties, Hamas, you'll have to wait another week, because I'm fertile," she told him, pushing him away. "You've seen how fertile my family is, how many of my brothers serve in your ranks, and how many of my sisters have been killed. Unless you are prepared to bear a child with me."

Deker watched her eyes drift up to him in the pergola for a moment.

"Tell me, Hamas. Would you feed your own son to Molech?"

"My son? No. My daughter? Without a second thought."

"Well, you know how it works." Rahab was all business. "I'm the sacred prostitute priestess who brings forth the crops, the crops bring the money and the money keeps everything going. I'm no good to anybody if I'm with child, and even that is but one burnt offering to Molech."

Hamas put his rough hand to her lovely throat and said, "The harvest is already here, and so are Bin-Nun's spies. Tell me what you did for them, or I'll snap your neck like the stem of a desert flower."

Deker's grip tightened around his sword, his eyes locked onto hers. She showed no fear, but her eyes widened as she looked over Hamas' shoulders and saw him move quietly on the pergola roof. Striking Hamas would mean the end of him and his mission to Jericho. But his feelings for Rahab were an irresistible force of nature he could not control. He simply had to protect her—in the way he failed to protect Rachel. He was emotionally and spiritually committed, and there was no turning back, regardless of the consequences.

But her eyes signaled to him that she was still in control and to back off. He paused, aware of a drop of perspiration rolling down his arm to his hands and the grip of the sword. It trickled down the blade to the point. Any second it would drop on them and reveal his presence above.

"Yes, the men came to me, but I didn't know where they came from," she said. "They left before you arrived, at dusk, when the city gate closed."

Hamas removed his hand from her neck, but seemed in no hurry to get off her. "What did they say?"

"They claimed to be jewelry traders. Asked about the city population. How many pieces of jewelry they could sell. Thought if I bought some and the girls wore them that maybe our customers would buy some for their wives."

"What did you say?"

"I didn't think wives would want to wear the same jewelry as their husband's whores."

Hamas gave a low, deep-throated laugh. "And then?"

"Then they said we could tell the husbands to tell their wives that their jewelry was magic and could make them fertile, or even to make them only conceive boys."

Hamas shook his head and finally stood up, apparently satisfied. "Hebrew magic," he complained. "They never stop stealing from us Egyptians. That's why we'll slaughter them. I think like Bin-Nun. I know what he wants."

"What is that?" Rahab asked as she adjusted her wrap and looked up at Hamas. Deker could tell she was trying not to look at him on the pergola.

"Bin-Nun wants to know if his magic act of fear has seized the imagination of our population," Hamas told her, and turned to help himself to some grapes on the table below Deker. "And, thanks to you and these spies of his, he now does. They'll report this and he'll decide to try to cross the Jordan even at flood stage and surprise us. He won't attack right away but will just sit on our trade routes, starve us out and then come in."

"You know this?"

"My spies and scouts tell me that for the past two months Bin-Nun has had his stonecutters building a bridge of stepping-stones across one of the fords in the Jordan. I even know their line of march. It's going to take three days to cross."

Rahab grew still. "You're going to attack the Israelites."

"When they're at their most vulnerable," Hamas said. "I'm going to let Bin-Nun get half his people over. Then, when they're split in two, half on the east bank and half on the west bank, we strike."

"'We'?"

"I'm going to kill their head, and then Moabite raiders will slay their tail in retribution for the slaughter of their women at the hands of the Levites," Hamas announced. "Then we'll finally rid this land of these locusts and I can accomplish what my parents' pharaoh failed to do."

Deker could see the scenario that Hamas described vividly. He drew his sword back just a bit, overwhelmed with a desire to kill this swine right now, when the drop from the tip of his blade fell to the bowl and splashed softly on a grape.

In that instant Rahab spoke loudly. "And if that doesn't work?"

Hamas didn't seem to notice the splash or turn his face up to the pergola roof. Instead he picked another grape and stuffed it into his mouth and turned to Rahab.

"I have a plan to save us in case we fail," he mumbled with his mouth full. "Nothing I'd be stupid enough to share with you. Where did these spies say they were going?"

"They didn't," she replied. "I don't know which way they went. But from what you said, it seems plain that they're going straight for the Jordan to report back to Bin-Nun. Think you can catch up with them?"

"They're dead already," he promised her as he walked out of view and Deker heard a door open. Before it closed behind him, Hamas added, "Next time I see you, my flower, I'll eat the sweeter fruit."

20

It was a shell game as Rahab moved Deker from room to room, avoiding any Reahn soldiers until they finally reached the ground floor. There Rahab pulled back an ornate rug to reveal a trapdoor and stone steps. He followed her down the narrow steps to the cellar below her villa.

Dust filtered down between the creaking wooden planks above, and Deker could hear the boots of the Reahn troops doing room checks. He looked down at the beaten earth below his boots and noticed it sloped upward to a small dark square in the far wall.

"This way," she told him.

Rahab's oil lamp illuminated a square tunnel opening in the wall. The bronze grillwork that had covered it lay on the floor.

They ducked through the short tunnel that led to a larger cellar filled with grains and rows of ceremonial jars. Then Deker saw the human skulls on the wall with seashells for eyes. The faces had been made up with lime to create some semblance of life.

"My other sisters," Rahab said calmly, and continued on her

way. "The jars have the smaller bones of newborns burned alive to Molech."

Between the strange odor of the preservatives in the jars and the scent of plants to mask it, Deker felt ill.

"Your way out," she said, pointing to the dark end of the room.

Wooden steps rose up to a small alcove and a window, and Deker realized this cellar was actually inside the outer city wall. A shadow moved next to the window and a voice startled him.

"I'll take the cruel justice of Shittim to this so-called civilization any day," said Elezar. He was already fastening a rope to the window while the girl who had taken him below looked on. "What took you so long?"

Then Elezar saw Rahab in the light, still holding Deker's hand, and did a double take at the resemblance to Rachel.

"Rahab," Deker told him. "She's coming with us."

"No, I'm not," she said, and Deker felt her yank away her hand. "I have family here. Hamas will kill them in retribution as an example to all in Reah for my betrayal."

Elezar tested the rope and seemed satisfied. "You heard the whore."

Elezar said it in English, but Rahab got the drift.

"Abraham is my forefather too," Rahab said in Hebrew, surprising Elezar. "And as Yahweh made a blood provision for Abraham to sacrifice instead of his son Isaac, so he will make provision for non-Hebrews."

"What do you know of Yahweh?" Elezar spat back.

"I know that forty years ago Yahweh sent the Angel of Death to Egypt, and today he has sent Bin-Nun to Reah," she said. "But

Hebrews were spared if they painted their doorposts with blood and the Angel of Death passed over them. I want to be passed over too. So I beg you, swear to me by Yahweh, since I have shown you kindness, that you also will show kindness to me and my house. Give me a true token, and spare my father, my mother, my brothers and all that they have, and deliver our lives from death when you destroy Jericho."

"No," said Elezar.

"She's saving our asses, Elezar," Deker shot back, and then told her, "Our lives for your lives."

"Two conditions," Elezar added in Aramaic, glaring at her. "One, neither you nor your family nor any of your sluts break your promise and talk about this business."

She nodded.

"Two, expect no kindness from us until after the Lord has given us the land."

She nodded again, and as she did they could feel the walls shake.

"What the hell is going on?" Elezar demanded.

"They're opening the gate for Hamas," she told them.

Deker stuck his head out the window and looked down the north wall twenty meters to the ground. The sound was coming from his right, and he looked east in time to see Hamas and his horsemen thunder out the main gate, only thirty meters or so out of view around the corner on the eastern wall. They were taking the main road toward the fords of the Jordan. Then the walls began to shake as the city gate closed again. Deker glanced up toward the top of the wall. The angle prevented him from seeing any Reahn guards, and hopefully the situation was the same for them.

He pulled his head back into the cellar and told Elezar, "We're good to go."

"Hamas and his riders will be scouring the fords up and down the Jordan," Rahab told them. "Hide in the hills to the north for a few days. Hamas will think he missed you and return. Then it will be safe for you to cross over."

Elezar looked noncommittal, refusing to confirm or deny any of their plans with her. Then he spoke to Deker in English. "We go for the Cave of Temptation. No more than a couple of kilometers from here. We hide out and then report back."

Deker nodded. The cave was allegedly the place where in coming centuries Jesus Christ fasted and prayed for forty days when he was tempted by the devil. By the sixth century, various monasteries and churches had been built over the entrance. By the twenty-first century it was a major tourist attraction in modern Jericho. The tram left from practically where he was standing inside the city and floated directly to the cave entrance. Tonight they'd have to take a more circuitous route.

Rahab said, "Now give me a sure sign that you will save us from death."

"The sign will be that you're still alive after we lay waste to your city and leave it on the ash heap of history," Elezar said, positioning himself in the window to rappel down the wall outside. "Deker, let's go."

Deker looked her in the eye. "Your lives for our lives."

She nodded.

Elezar shook his head. "I hope she's fucking worth it, Deker," he said, and disappeared out the window.

It was now just him and Rahab left in the cellar, along with the quiet girl in the corner who had been invisible the entire time.

"Hamas will suspect you lied to him," Deker told Rahab. "Come with us."

"No," she said. "You come back for me."

She looked at him in a way that told him that she had been saving her soul for him all along, even if she had been unable to save her body. Then she kissed him on the mouth and wrapped her arms around him and squeezed him tight.

Something was released in Deker at that moment, a primal desire to love and protect her, body and soul, no matter what. Like he had always wanted to love and protect Rachel. He didn't want to let go of her, but knew he couldn't protect her unless he did.

"I will," he promised as he moved to the window.

The wind had died down and the desert was an empty sea. Holding the rope, he climbed over the ledge backward, feet planted against the wall below the window until he was staring back inside at Rahab.

"Don't worry about the rope," she told him. "I'll pull it up as soon as you reach the bottom."

Deker hesitated, the nagging sense that he was forgetting something. Something was off here, but he couldn't put his finger on it. But time was running out.

He rappelled down the outside of the city wall, stopping twice on the way down. Seconds later his feet hit the ground and he was staring at the concrete revetment wall at the bottom. But there was no sign of Elezar, who had already taken off for the hills.

He gave the rope two sharp tugs and watched it disappear into the dark somewhere beyond view.

He took off into the darkness. Only once did he stop and look back at the city, trying to pick out which window among several in the north wall was Rahab's. But he wasn't sure.

Suddenly he realized what he had forgotten and Elezar most certainly had not.

The scarlet cord.

They were supposed to have told Rahab to tie a red scarf in her window as a sign to General Bin-Nun. *Her rear cellar window in the city wall.* Without that sign, the invading Israelite troops wouldn't know which portion of the walls, let alone which home inside, to spare.

Rahab was already dead.

21

The clouds had parted and the moon shone down on Deker like a beacon as he crossed the fields toward the cliffs of the Mount of Temptation. At any moment he expected a horn to sound and a rain of arrows to strike him down, or to fall into one of the many trenches dug around the city. But in less than twenty minutes he reached a pomegranate grove and could hear the roar of a creek at the base of the cliffs. He found the narrow goats' path up the side of the mountain, but no Elezar.

Deker swore and started his steep and winding hike along the eastern slope. A couple of times his boot slipped and he heard a waterfall of stones cascade down the cliff. The higher he climbed, the more he could see of the desert moonscape and Jericho below. All the while he thought of Elezar's betrayal, seething with rage.

There were a few dozen caves, and it took Deker an additional fifteen minutes to find Elezar by a small fire deep inside one of the larger caves. Elezar didn't even bother to look to see who entered, although he cocked his ear when Deker removed the sword from his sheath.

"So young Deker didn't completely forget his years of Hebrew school back in the States," Elezar said in a calm and even voice.

"The scarlet cord, Elezar," Deker said, putting the tip of his blade to the back of Elezar's neck. "We were supposed to tell her to put one of her red scarves in her outside window, to mark her house for invading troops to spare. You left out that little detail. You left her to die for no other reason but your self-righteous religious sanctimony."

Elezar stiffened only slightly. "Six million reasons, Deker. Six million Jews."

"What are you talking about?"

"The book of Matthew lists Rahab as part of the human lineage of Jesus," Elezar said. "No Rahab, no Jesus. No Jesus, no Christianity. No Christianity, no Crusades, no Nazis, no Holocaust."

Deker paused, horrified at Elezar's logic.

"You're assuming that those who do evil in the name of Christ in the future won't simply create another religion to justify their slaughter of Jews," Deker said. "You think that by letting Rahab get slaughtered you're going to prevent the Holocaust? You don't know that. But you do know that she's also the great-great-grandmother of King David. You're going to murder Israel's greatest king and erase the Psalms from history. You're insane!"

Elezar sat calmly, tending to the fire with a small stick. "Rahab corrupted and poisoned Israel. You know this now just from the blazing star. The emblem of Israel isn't even Jewish, confirming what Moses and Bin-Nun feared all along: the Israelites will conquer the Promised Land, only to take up the religious practices of its enemies. We can stop the infection now, before it enters our nation's bloodstream. God deposed Saul and raised David. He can always find another king of the Jews. And we can make new Psalms. You said it yourself, Deker: if this is really happening, if we are really back in time, then history has already been changed. We make the most of it."

"This is so wrong, Elezar."

"No, Deker. This is the cry of six million Jews thanking us. This is God's judgment on the Amorites or Reahns or whatever they want to call themselves. You saw the whoredom, the oppression and the infanticide. It's been building for four centuries. We just happen to be the hand of God like the angels that nuked Sodom and Gomorrah. We have been chosen. You should be grateful."

Deker stepped around Elezar toward the fire, slowly drawing a white scratch with the tip of his blade across Elezar's neck until its point rested at his throat. The slightest drop of blood formed out of the line where the skin had broken.

"You make a mockery of our national character," Deker said. "She trusted us, Elezar. She trusted Yahweh. She has more faith than any of you hypocrites. We gave her our word. We gave her our word, and now our word is worth shit. You betrayed our people, Elezar. You will make the world hate us."

Elezar looked up at Deker, fire in his eyes. "I'm saving our nation both now and in the future, Deker," he said defiantly. "But you would show less devotion to your Jewish brothers than your foreign whores."

It was all Deker could do to hold himself back. "Damn you, Elezar. You know that little prick Phineas is going to run a blade through her if Hamas doesn't beat him to it."

Elezar said nothing, and silence filled the cave.

Then came the crunch of pebbles outside the entrance, and instantly they went on guard.

"Hear that?" Elezar asked, cocking his ear.

Deker nodded. "Could be goats."

"Or the sound of your beloved's betrayal."

Elezar kicked dirt on the fire, and they quietly made their way to the mouth of the cave and looked outside.

"There," Elezar said, pointing.

Immediately beneath them on the winding trail, a line of soldiers was moving toward their cave. Were it not for the glint of their spears in the moonlight, they would have been invisible against the cliffs.

Deker said, "The famous shadow army?"

"Doesn't matter," Elezar said. "I told you she'd betray us."

22

Deker edged close to the cave's entrance and looked out. The troops with their torches were already halfway up the narrow path toward the cave. Another unit was coming down from the top of the mountain, where the Reahns maintained an outpost. He and Elezar were sandwiched in between.

"We break into the open and we're dead," Deker whispered, listening to the voices of the troops as they drew near. "What does it mean 'to feed them to Molech'?"

"It means they're going to turn this cave into an oven and burn us alive," Elezar told him. "If we stay here, they could fry us."

"I don't think we have a choice." Deker peered back into the dark cave. "How far back does this cave go?"

But Elezar had already vanished.

Deker felt his way along the cave walls, penetrating deeper and deeper into the mountain. The farther he went, the colder it got. He found Elezar hunched over a small crawl hole from which Deker felt an even colder blast of air.

"Now we're animals crawling through holes," Deker told him.

Elezar said nothing and disappeared into the hole as the illumination of torches and the sound of voices behind him grew closer.

"There!" shouted one of the Reahns, and the ground began to shake as the entire unit raced toward the back of the cave.

Deker dove into the hole as splashes of some tar-like substance hit his feet and slowed him down. Slithering as fast as he could, he looked back in time to see a torch at the mouth of the hole.

"They're in Molech's Maze," a Reahn said, his voice echoing through the narrow hole. "Any volunteers?"

There were none.

"Then we feed them to Molech."

The torch touched the mouth of the hole, and a giant fireball erupted and started chasing Deker through the tunnel. Soon the fissure sloped down, and he started sliding uncontrollably down the chute. He landed in the bottom of a larger cave as a blast of fire shot over his head and singed his hair.

Deker took a deep breath and coughed in the smoky air. He tried to get his bearings before searching for Elezar. He might have escaped the frying pan only to land in the fire. The Reahn scouts obviously called it Molech's Maze for a reason: a man could get lost in these caves and never come out.

"Elezar!" he called out.

There was no response.

He started moving farther into the mountain, because he couldn't go back the way he came in. A deep sense of doubt began to torment him. What if his infiltration and escape from Jericho were all for naught? What if he failed to return to Bin-Nun with his intel on Hamas' plot to hit the Israelites as they crossed the Jordan? They could be slaughtered as soon as they touched foot on the west bank. What if he didn't get back to Rahab before the Israelites hit Jericho? She'd die with the rest of the Reahns, and with her the Psalms of David and future kings of Israel.

Deker prayed for the first time in a long while that this would not be the case. That Yahweh would reveal himself to him now.

Deker was now aware of another presence in the cave with him. A large presence, bigger than a man. He could hear the deep, groaning breath of some creature. Slowly the outline of a shape became clearer as his eyes adjusted to the darkness, and Deker saw a giant hairy head with red eyes staring back at him from the face of a bull.

It was Molech incarnate.

23

Deker pulled out his sword and swung at Molech, sending the head of the bull floating away down the cave on two legs. But this Molech was slow and wobbly, and Deker soon tackled him to the dirt. He pulled off the bull's head and saw the ravaged face of a Reahn soldier, or rather a former soldier. It looked like the man had tried to cut away a military tattoo from his shoulder.

"Who are you?" Deker demanded in ancient Hebrew.

The man's eyes went wide, but not in fear. He began blabbering in the dialect of the Reahns, but Deker couldn't understand him.

"He wants to know if you're really a Hebrew," said a voice from behind that Deker immediately recognized as Elezar's.

"And where the hell have you been?" Deker demanded.

Elezar stepped forward with a torch. "Finding an exit. There's a cave that leads out the back of the mountain and down into a valley. It will take us a day to reach the Jordan, but if we avoid the Reahn scouts at the fords, we should be able to swim across and make it back to Shittim by the following day."

The would-be Molech nodded slowly to confirm to Deker what Elezar said.

Elezar bent over the man and examined him under the light of his torch. "This man is dying," Elezar said. "Look at his pupils, his pale-blue skin. No wonder the Reahn army cut him loose. We should let him die and go our way."

"A little late for that," Deker said, and shoved the man up into a seated position against the cave wall. "Ask him what he's doing running around playing Molech."

Elezar exchanged words with the man, who grew animated as he spoke quickly and waved his hands until he tired and they fell to his sides. Then the words came more slowly but clearly.

"He says his name is Saleh," Elezar translated. "General Hamas forced him to wear this real, hollowed-out head of a bull and roam the caves to scare local villagers so that in times of trouble they would avoid seeking refuge here and instead turn to the walls of Jericho for protection."

Deker asked, "And what did this guy do to deserve this kind of duty?"

"Saleh says nothing. Hamas raped his wife and then offered up the daughter she bore to the great statue of Molech inside Jericho. The daughter was burned in the temple ovens. Then Hamas made Saleh a digger in the trenches outside Jericho where they leave the sick and the dead to rot until the sun peels the skin off their bones. He did this for months until one day there were no more sick—besides himself, at that point."

Deker frowned. "What do you mean? There are always sick people."

"Not in Jericho anymore," Elezar said. "According to Saleh, Hamas proclaimed that Molech had healed all the sick and blessed Jericho with divine health and prosperity. That's when Hamas sent Saleh to work the caves for the sake of the straggling believers in the outer valley. To keep them more scared of Molech than Yahweh. He is glad to see that the army of Yahweh has finally arrived and that at last the disease of Molech will be destroyed."

At that moment Saleh grabbed Deker by the shoulders with his gnarled hands and looked at him with his pale eyes, the light of life visibly fading. He babbled something unintelligible before his hands weakened and let go of Deker.

"He said to burn the Reahns," Elezar said. "Burn them all to hell."

24

By noon the next day Deker and Elezar had safely crossed the Jordan and made it back to Shittim. After a quick debrief with old Caleb, some rest and supper, Deker sat silently in the command tent while Elezar delivered his assessment of Hamas and the morale of his troops to General Bin-Nun and his top forty officers.

"Yahweh has surely given the whole land into our hands," said Elezar, concluding his official report. "All the people are melting in fear because of us."

Not a word about Rahab, Deker thought, but that would be remedied soon enough. He would do everything in his power to persuade Bin-Nun to send them back to Jericho before any attack. He had to get back to Rahab and make things right for her—and Israel.

It was the junior spy's turn now, and as Elezar turned the presentation over to Deker he fixed his gaze with a look that warned him not to make trouble. God's holy angels could not be split in their report, because heaven was not a house divided, and Bin-Nun wasn't looking for anything other than a rubber stamp for his invasion.

This much had been obvious to Deker as soon as they had reached the Judah Gate at the western entrance to the camp. The Judah Division had been at the eastern end of the camp when they had left for Jericho. While they were gone Bin-Nun had rearranged the order of the camp and troops, pitching it toward Jericho. But he had kept the signal tower with its cloud by day and fire by night east of the camp to fool both the Moabites and Reahns into thinking the camp was still pitched toward Mount Nebo. In so doing, he had shaved a good two or three days off their prep time in breaking down the camp to move out in battle column.

Deker stood up before the clay model of Jericho that he had made. With a thin rod he pointed to and explained the fortifications of Jericho, detailing the composition of the walls, depth, height and defenses.

"You saw what I did with my magic mud bricks to the old stone monument," he began, and got nods and murmurs of approval from some of the commanders, although Bin-Nun and his defense contractor Kane remained stone-faced. "I can do the same to the walls of Jericho."

"But what are your mud bricks against those great walls?" asked Salmon from the back of the tent. He was standing in the outer ring of aides, who were supposed to be seen and not heard; but his offense was taken in stride, as it seemed to be the thought on all the commanders' minds.

"I only have to blow out a section of the wall for you to enter, not the whole thing, and I've got enough mud bricks. It's like cutting a tree to make it fall in a particular direction. Let me show you."

He took his rod and tapped a spot on the north side of the upper fortress wall that he had specially prepared. The section fell like a drawbridge over the tops of the roofs to the lower city wall. Then he tapped the top of that lower wall and it, too, fell like a drawbridge to the reed mat.

There were murmurs all around, and a clear desire for further explanation.

"We don't have to bring down all the walls to enter the city," he told them. "Two pinpoint blasts—one in a weak section of the upper fortress wall and another in the lower city wall—will do the trick. The first blast will not only open the upper fortress wall, it will bring down the bricks on top of the buildings below like an avalanche, all the way down to the city wall. It may even be enough to smash through the lower city wall. But just in case, I will have a second blast to blow that wall in two. The bricks that spill down to the ground will create a slope that will enable you to climb over the lower revetment wall and into the city. From there you can climb straight up into the fortress, one after the other."

The commanders were amazed and delighted.

All except for Bin-Nun.

"You still have not solved the problem of gaining entrance to the city to plant your explosives," the general said. "By your own assessments, the walls are insurmountable, and you'll never pass through the main gate again. You fooled the guards once. But you can be sure they won't make that mistake again, or Hamas will make them pay for it with their lives."

Deker glanced at Elezar, who instantly knew where he was going, and warned him with his eyes not to go there. "There is another way, General," he said. "A way to pass through the walls."

Bin-Nun stared at him and told his commanders, "Leave us."

25

One by one the commanders cleared the tent, none looking back, until besides him there was only Bin-Nun, Elezar and Salmon, whom Bin-Nun allowed to remain.

Deker cleared his throat and said, "I was with the granddaughter of the woman who gave you refuge in Canaan forty years ago. I gave her the necklace her grandmother gave you before she died."

Bin-Nun closed his eyes. Elezar stared.

"Her name, too, is Rahab, and as her grandmother did for you, so Rahab gave us refuge and helped us escape Jericho. In return, I promised that we would spare her life and those of her family."

Elezar said nothing but did not dispute it, including their promise to spare her.

"Through her window in the north wall of Jericho, Elezar and I can get back into the city and plant the explosives," Deker said.

"If she doesn't betray us," Elezar finally chimed in. "There could be a contingent of Reahn soldiers waiting for us. We can't trust a whore."

"She saved our lives," Deker cut in.

"By lying to her authorities," Elezar shot back. "She is neither truthful nor trustworthy."

Bin-Nun seemed to wrestle with it for a moment, but then shook his head.

"Elezar is right. It's too risky. I cannot afford to let you go back and get caught. Before, you knew little. Now you know much. If you are captured, Hamas would have you, your explosives and our plans."

"Rahab can be trusted," Deker insisted. "Thanks to her, I learned Hamas' secret plan to destroy you."

Bin-Nun looked dubious. "Everybody has a secret plan to destroy us. How do I know this plan is real?"

"The plan is as real as the secret bridge you've built," Deker said, fixing his gaze on Bin-Nun.

The haunted look that Deker had seen in the general's eyes before he blew the dolmen monument had returned as soon as Deker said *secret bridge.*

"Hamas knows you're going to cross the Jordan at flood stage and not wait," Deker explained. "He also knows that, even with the secret bridge you've built, it will take three days for all Israel to cross."

Elezar stared, speechless for once.

"Hamas intends to bait you for a day and then attack when Israel is only halfway across, General," Deker went on. "He's got the Moabites lined up to wipe out the rear here on the east bank."

Bin-Nun was quiet, all his plans flushed. Elezar was amazed, either because of the quality of the intel or because Deker hadn't played the card until now.

"But we can help you, General," Deker assured him. "You show me this bridge you've built, and I'll show you how I can get Israel across in one day. Then it will be too late for Hamas to attack you when you're at half strength, and the Jordan will fall behind you like a wall to protect your rear from the Moabites. Then you'll let me return to Jericho through Rahab's window and bring down its walls."

26

"Looks like wonders have finally ceased, Elezar."

Deker and Elezar stood with Caleb, Salmon and Achan on the east bank of the Jordan under the stars, just a stone's throw from the forward base and stone table where Caleb had first given them their instructions to spy out Jericho. Now they saw the secret ford that Caleb and his stonecutters had been hiding all along.

"It's an Irish bridge," a shocked and dismayed Elezar said out loud.

"I see the bridge," Deker said. "What makes it Irish?"

"During the British Mandate of Palestine in the early twentieth century, Irish engineers in the British army breached dry riverbeds with concrete blocks that would survive the spring floods and allow vehicles to cross over," Elezar explained. "That's what Bin-Nun's army corps of engineers seem to have done here."

Deker was impressed. Caleb's stonecutters had constructed their own ford across the bottom of the Jordan by layering one stone atop another to build it up under the water's surface. Then they topped the whole thing off with twelve massive dolmen slabs, each about seven meters long. In so doing, they had created a platform wide and long enough for forty thousand troops and their families to cross the Jordan.

"So much for the parting of the Jordan, Elezar," he said. "This explains how the book of Joshua claims that the priests who bore the Ark of the Covenant stood on dry land in the middle of the Jordan until all the people had finished crossing the Jordan."

Elezar reluctantly had to agree, but still managed to look down his self-righteous nose at Deker with a glare. Elezar was still steaming over Deker's "dishonorable circumvention" of his authority back at camp by revealing the deal with Rahab. That Elezar learned of the secret Hamas plan to cut them off at the river at the same time as everybody else only further infuriated him. "You're untruthful, Deker," he had fumed. "And you cannot be trusted."

Neither, it seemed, could Bin-Nun.

"Bin-Nun leaves nothing to chance," said Salmon from behind, and with more than a hint of bitterness. "Nor to Yahweh."

Salmon and Achan must have known about the bridge all along. Yet another reason for Bin-Nun to sub him and Elezar for the Jericho mission in case they were captured and talked.

"Maybe," said Deker. "But your bridge runs below the surface of the water. Your engineers miscalculated how high the Jordan would rise at flood stage."

The Jordan had a zigzag current where its shallowest depths were in the middle. The center of the bridge actually broke the surface of the water every now and then, but it was clear the flooding was worse than even Bin-Nun had accounted for, and much of the bridge was a good meter underwater.

"The swift current is a concern to the Levites carrying the Ark," said a squeaky voice.

Deker turned to see Phineas, who seemed to have perfected the art of creeping up silently and unannounced. "If anything were to happen, it would break the morale of the people even before they set foot in the Promised Land."

"I don't know, Phineas," Deker said. "It would be a shame to see the Ark float down the Jordan. But I'd rather enjoy watching you slip and fall on your fat ass."

Achan started to laugh but caught himself, assuming the stern look of the others.

"We crossed the cliffs and canyons of the Wadi Zered to reach Shittim," insisted old Caleb, who seemed to read Deker's concern. "We can get all forty army contingents and forty thousand women and children across the Jordan. But it will take longer than the three days we allotted. The current is faster than we anticipated, and the floodwaters higher."

Caleb was waiting on him now for some kind of answer.

"You get Kane to give me back my C-4, and I can get you all over the Jordan in one day," Deker said.

"One day?" Caleb repeated.

Deker drew a groove in the ground with a stick to represent the Jordan. Then he put a rock in the center to represent the bridge.

"In the American West, when a family wanted to cross a river, they brought their wagon upstream to break the current," he said, knowing full well Caleb didn't know what the hell he was referring to. But the old man got the idea. "We do the same upstream—say, at Adam, where the Jordan narrows. By blowing some rocks and caving the banks, we can dam the Jordan. That will slow the current, drop the water level and let you cross on dry ground, or bridge, so to speak."

Caleb and Phineas looked at each other for a moment and then slowly nodded. Salmon and Achan could not argue with the logic either. Elezar said nothing, but seemed to burn in anger at him all the same.

"Now you'll still camp on the banks for three days, but you'll cross over in one," Deker explained. "When Hamas sees your pillar of fire jump the Jordan that first night he's going to shit his own bricks and call off his attack."

"And if he doesn't?" Caleb pressed.

"At least you'll have your full army to fight."

Caleb was almost convinced, but not quite. "What about the Moabites hitting our rear guard?"

"As soon as your last man is across the Jordan, you'll send units back to haul out those dolmen slabs from the dry riverbed," Deker said. "As soon as you send up a pillar of smoke to signal you're all on the west bank, I'll detonate a second blast up in Adam to blow the dam I created with the first blast. That will release the floodwaters of the Jordan again. The force of that wave will wipe away what's left of your bridge and drop a wall of water between you and the Moabites, keeping them where they belong on the east bank. It will also keep your people on the west bank from going wobbly when you attack Jericho. Because there will be no going back."

Caleb and the rest seemed to follow what he was saying, at least the gist of it.

"This is the divine plan of Yahweh," Phineas announced conclusively, almost reverently. "I will take this to Bin-Nun. He will tell the commanders to prepare the people to move out tomorrow. The Levites will lead the way."

"This is not the plan," Salmon angrily muttered.

"Good," said Deker, ignoring Salmon and addressing Phineas. "And you'll remind General Bin-Nun that he has Rahab the harlot to thank for this plan."

Elezar, however, was anything but pleased with the plan, though apparently for different reasons than Salmon. He saved his wrath for Deker until they were alone.

"You're a liar, Deker," he said. "You pretend to be ignorant of Scripture and then propose we dam the Jordan at Adam. The book of Joshua says that's exactly what miraculously happened, perhaps thanks to an earthquake."

"Or maybe the Israelites threw some boulders in," Deker said, adding, "Really, I didn't know."

"Tell me then how you came up with the idea," Elezar pressed, refusing to let it go. "I suppose Yahweh personally presented it to you?"

"Maybe," Deker said. "My first year in the IDF, drought caused the Jordan River to recede to a level never seen before. This caused boulders to appear beside the Adam Bridge. It looked like a dam. Jordan accused Israel of stopping the flow of water so Israeli farmers could irrigate their crops while farms and tourism on Jordan's side of the river withered."

Elezar's angry eyes widened slightly, revealing he indeed recalled hearing something about the water crisis that had flared briefly between Israel and Jordan.

"I was dispatched to Adam with earthmoving equipment and explosives if necessary to clear stones from the river and prove to the Jordanians that Israel wasn't at fault," Deker continued.

"And what happened?" Elezar demanded.

"We cleared the rocks but the water still didn't flow. That proved to everybody that the real issue was the farmland on both sides of the river. It was siphoning off the water and causing the drought, turning the Jordan into the sick trickle of a stream that you and I know in our own time," Deker said. "Still, I always had my doubts about how the stones got there in the first place."

"And now, I suppose, you know for certain?"

"Yes, I do," Deker told him. "I put them there."

27

The next morning Deker and Elezar, along with the Judah Division officers Salmon and Achan, left the camp at Shittim and headed toward Adam. The small town was a good seventeen kilometers upstream from Shittim and a full day's march. So they rode on camels instead of horses to cut the number of times they had to stop for water.

The entire area was controlled by the Israelite tribe of Gad, which was going to commit its troops to the crossing into Canaan but keep the land east of the Jordan. Deker thought the choice ill-advised, as the Gadites would forever expose themselves to attack on three sides, whereas the tribes that crossed the Jordan and settled in Canaan would have the river to their east and mountains all around as natural barriers.

But it wasn't worth the fight to second-guess a Gadite. That much Deker could tell halfway along the march when they watered their camels at a small town in the low plains called Beth-Nimrah. More than two hundred armed Gadites were waiting to escort them the rest of the way to Adam. Big, burly warriors with rough beards and sheepskin caps, the Gadites clearly helped Bin-Nun's army flex its muscle wherever it went. Their torn tunics looked like rags on their swarthy physiques, which revealed a definite penchant for body piercings but, oddly, no tattoos.

Deker had tried to explain to Bin-Nun back at Shittim that this was going to be a small operation. But Bin-Nun would have none of it, insisting on a full contingent of Gadites to assist Deker in damming the Jordan at Adam. Furthermore, Bin-Nun had also insisted on not allowing Deker to carry his C-4 but instead entrusting the bricks to Achan and the detonators to Salmon.

Only if they succeeded with the dam would Bin-Nun reconsider sending Deker on to Jericho with the rest of the C-4 that Kane the Kenite was holding on to. Such was the trust Deker had inspired with the general after his successful spy mission in Jericho.

Some things never changed.

"So I hear you got some milk and honey in the Promised Land," Achan said, riding up on his camel beside him after they left the town. "And I hear she's got money too."

The young Judean was starting to amuse Deker as a comic foil to his big and sober friend Salmon, who was leading the line at the front with Elezar and one of the Gadites.

Deker dodged the question with a wink and asked, "Salmon still have a bug up his ass because he wasn't the first to cross the Jordan?"

"He thinks that General Bin-Nun has shown no faith in Yahweh by following your plan."

"So we should wait for the waters to dam themselves at Adam?"

"If Bin-Nun wants the people to see that Yahweh's favor rests on him as with Moses, yes," Achan said. "Salmon believes you are stealing Yahweh's thunder with your magic mud bricks."

"Is that all?" Deker asked.

"He also says that the blazing star you wear proves we're doomed. That we may well conquer the Promised Land, only to fall into the same evil as those whom Yahweh has brought judgment upon. Salmon's feelings run deep like the Jordan."

For a moment Deker was tempted to give Achan some consolation to share with his good friend Salmon. But whatever else he was, he was no liar.

"You got that right," Deker said, and watched Achan's face fall. "Tell Salmon I've seen the future of Israel, and this blazing star is it. Unless he prefers no future at all."

Achan's shoulders slumped and they rode on in gloomy silence.

Deker knew he could have spun a tale of a victorious future for Israel. But as he gazed at the yawning, rocky desert all around, he knew Israel's future promised even more desolate wandering and backsliding than the past forty years in the Sinai Desert.

The same arid emptiness had swallowed his own soul long ago, Deker realized. His own pilgrimage to adulthood and later through several twenty-first-century wars had been marked by the same physical and spiritual wanderings as these Hebrews. He, too, had been prone to pursue anything but the faith of his fathers, intent instead to carve his own way through the world, consequences be damned.

Now he wondered if his own future was as bleak as Israel's, even if he ultimately did succeed in saving Rahab and razing the walls of Jericho. For the first time, he could appreciate Salmon's angst. To win a war and lose your soul was no victory at all. Only his thoughts of Rachel's and Rahab's common faith in Yahweh gave him a sliver of encouragement. They saw hope for a world he had long thought hopeless, even if their hope wasn't in humanity itself but in the mercy of the Creator who made them. Too bad the Creator had also apparently left them all to kill one another and make a hell on earth.

Deker began to blink in the harsh glare of the sun as dust caked his face and sweat stung his burning eyes. They stopped briefly to water the camels and snack on wild figs. But there was little small talk, even among the Gadites. Every man seemed content to stay silent in his own thoughts, and Deker was no exception.

The hours wore on and the sun dropped low until at last they came to Adam. The settlement wasn't much to look at—a dozen widely dispersed huts with fire pits and pens for animals—and if Deker had blinked he would have missed it. Then they passed over a ridge between two hills at dusk to behold a massive field of dolmen monuments next to a narrow bend in the Jordan River. In the center was a small cluster of tents around a fire, where forty or so Gadites had pitched camp for them.

Deker stared at the acres of dolmens all around. It was as if he were in the middle of Arlington National Cemetery, surrounded by thousands of tombstones. Suddenly Deker understood. The Gadites weren't there to help him blow the riverbanks with his explosives. They were there in case he failed. They'd simply dam the waters with the dolmens.

Salmon saw it too, and brought his camel around to Deker, scowling all the way over.

"Behold the great faith of General Joshua bin-Nun," Salmon said. "He trusts in Yahweh, yet leaves nothing to chance."

28

The local Gadites greeted the arriving convoy with the sound of shouts and slinging of arrows into the air.

"What's all the fuss?" Deker asked Salmon.

"They're just blazing off for the hell of it," Salmon said. "An annoying waste of ammunition. I've come to my wit's end trying to explain to them that Kane's smiths aren't working night and day to manufacture arrowheads so they can shoot them off whenever they feel like it. But they consider themselves wild men of the mountains."

As they came down into the camp, more Gadites ran along beside them to take their camels. A fire burned in the center of the earthen floor, around which the arriving Gadites had clustered.

"Food!" Achan declared.

Deker saw that the Gadites had spread a rug on the ground in front of the fire for him and Elezar. A young Gadite offered him what looked like seasoned lamb sausage on a stick. The aroma, however, smelled foul to Deker and he politely declined.

"You insult them," Elezar said, joining the others in helping himself.

Deker sat down and looked around the circle at the rough faces and curious eyes fixed on him. He decided to pretend he was back at Pink's in Los Angeles and this lamb sausage was just a hot dog.

Gingerly he took the stick on which the sausage was speared and bit off one end. The first sensation was his tongue burning from the heat, but then the fat and spices exploded in his mouth and he realized these Gadite chefs could take on any Top Chef. Eagerly he devoured the sausage and accepted another.

He wasn't even halfway finished with his second before the Gadites peppered him and Elezar with questions.

"What's Bin-Nun doing down at Shittim?"

"When is the invasion coming?"

"Are you really angels of the Lord?"

Elezar cleared his throat. "Tomorrow we will cave in the banks of the Jordan to dam the waters. Then you will see the power of Yahweh."

At that moment a sullen Salmon marched up with the detonators in his fist. He held them over the fire as if he were about to drop them into the flames.

"Surely an angel of the Lord doesn't need trinkets like these to work a miracle," he said, his voice trembling.

Deker glanced at Elezar, who neither approved nor disapproved of what was happening. In Deker's mind, he was only encouraging the foolish Salmon. Slowly, Deker rose to his feet and faced Salmon.

"No," Deker told him, and then showed off his command of

ancient Hebrew after a week of total immersion. "But apparently you do, big man, to stand up to an angel."

Salmon's hand wavered over the flames. Any second Deker expected to see blisters forming on the skin.

An alarmed Achan said, "Give the angel his flints for his magic mud bricks, Salmon! We're under orders from Bin-Nun, under whom your father served."

"My father served Moses and the Lord God Yahweh!" Salmon cried out. "Moses needed no magic mud bricks, nor any angels to work miracles! He spoke to Yahweh face-to-face, and he parted the Red Sea with a stick!"

Deker eyed Salmon's white-red knuckles, looking for the first sign Salmon might let go. "Elezar, talk to me. What's going on?"

"Salmon is the son of Nahshon bin-Amminadab," Elezar said in ancient Hebrew, so Salmon could understand the angels knew his family well apart from Bin-Nun. "He is a direct descendant of Judah and the brother-in-law of Aaron, brother of Moses. When Moses stretched out his staff on the banks of the Red Sea and the waters did not part, Salmon's father entered the waters up to his nose and then the sea parted. This was more than twenty years before Salmon was born."

Deker now understood that Salmon had wanted to emulate his late father's exploits and place of honor among the Israelites, but that he and Elezar had preempted that dream with their arrival.

Salmon said, "Tell me, angel, is it true?"

"Is what true?" Deker asked.

"Everything our fathers told us," Salmon said. "The Exodus—the plagues, the parting of the Red Sea."

Elezar said, "Of course it's true, Salmon. Everything happened as your father said."

"Not you," Salmon said. "I'm asking the bad angel."

The bad angel.

Deker empathized with the young soldier. Everything Salmon had seen in the last few days—the bridge, the stones, the magic mud bricks, suspicious spies dubbed "angels"—was nothing at all like the Sunday-school stories Salmon, and Deker himself, had been taught growing up. Salmon's world as a refugee in the desert was so paltry and brutish compared to his father's big-budget Exodus, it was only natural for him to wonder if anything he had been taught ever happened.

"I wasn't there, Salmon," Deker said. "Elezar is your angel of ancient history. I know only the future—or did. Everything is a bit up in the air right now."

Deker in that instant dove over the fire and tackled Salmon, slamming the back of Salmon's hand with the detonators against the ground until the fist opened and they spilled out for Elezar to grab.

"I serve Yahweh, the God of my fathers!" Salmon screamed. "We all serve Yahweh! We need no angels!"

A fire log came down on Salmon's head, knocking him out. Holding it at the other end was Achan. Deker got the distinct impression this wasn't the first time Salmon had gone out like this.

Deker sighed, looking sadly at the poor man sprawled in the dirt. Deker could relate to Salmon. After all, he himself had been questioning reality ever since his escape in Madaba. How could he fault Salmon for doubting his own reality?

"Poor Salmon cannot compromise," Achan explained. "That's what makes him a warrior in battle but a fool around the fire."

29

The following day Deker watched Salmon wake up on the west bank of the Jordan and get his bearings. Salmon frowned when he saw where he was—in a grapevine hold around a sycamore tree—and that the dam had been made below. Deker, meanwhile, looked down the long, dry riverbed to the south, where seventeen kilometers away a column of smoke rose into the sky.

That was the signal from General Bin-Nun that the armies of Israel had successfully crossed over the Jordan.

"Congratulations, Salmon, you're on the other side," Deker told him, and offered him a fig. "The land of milk and honey. Want some?"

Salmon refused, seemingly determined to go on a hunger strike until he saw the hand of the Lord. "Have the Ark and the people crossed?"

"See for yourself." Deker pointed out the distant, distinctive pillar of smoke on the west bank. "I'm sure Phineas and his Levites dipped their toes in the Jordan as soon as the water table dropped below the top of the washout bridge."

"Some miracle," Salmon said in defeat.

"Yes. Actually, look over there at our dam." Deker pointed it out to him. "See the mud between the boulders? See the small waterfalls? It's beginning to break up under its own accord from the force of the water. I won't have to use my magic mud bricks after all. The Jordan will be back at flood stage in no time."

Deker himself was eager to reach the new Israelite camp, grab the rest of his C-4 and finally save Rahab and blow the walls of Jericho once and for all. Then history would be right again—and maybe Israel and himself too.

"'Our people,'" Salmon muttered. "What do you know about our people?"

"Only their future."

Salmon stared at the IDF dog tag with the Star of David emblem dangling from Deker's sunburnt neck. "I see the future in your Blazing Star. If that is the seal of Israel, then our future is as bleak as Bin-Nun feared. We will conquer the Promised Land only to be conquered by the false gods of foreigners."

"These foreigners are your cousins, Salmon, and some of them fear and worship Yahweh."

"Like this whore you spoke of with Bin-Nun?" Salmon seemed singularly unimpressed.

"Yes. Unlike you, this whore doesn't need to see the miraculous signs of Yahweh to believe. Her faith is greater than yours."

"You offend me."

"That's not too difficult," Deker said. "But don't worry. In three thousand years Israel will still have those like Phineas and Elezar to carry the Law around and enslave the people. Israel will still be surrounded by her enemies on all sides. People like Kane the Kenite will still give Israel weapons, even some that can incinerate cities in the blink of an eye like Sodom and Gomorrah."

They sat silently for a while watching the dam naturally break up from the pressure of the waters behind it. First the large chunks of mud broke off, and then came the waterfalls. The rocks would be swallowed up by the rising floodwaters and disappear.

Deker then helped untie the young Judean from his tree and get him to his feet. "Salmon, would you care to lead us to the new camp Bin-Nun is setting up in the Promised Land? Believe it or not, he wouldn't share the location with me in advance."

Deker's gesture seemed to pick up Salmon's spirit a bit, although the soldier tried not to show it over the course of the long and winding route they and the two hundred Gadites had to travel to avoid any trouble with long-range Reahn patrols.

The day wore on, slowly giving way to night. The convoy stopped to rest, the Gadites pulling out dried dates and flatbreads from their packs, and supplementing their meager meal with fresh figs and other fruits they pulled from surrounding trees. After an insufficient amount of time to sleep, they rose before dawn and pressed on toward the new Israelite camp.

As the horizon blazed red with dusk, they straggled down the rocky slope toward the Jordan and into the camp. Deker smelled smoke.

They passed over a ridge and saw the plains below. Deker immediately knew something was horribly wrong. Hundreds of columns of fire and smoke billowed up into the night above the sea of tents. The last time he had seen anything like it was during his first tour of duty with American forces in Iraq.

"We've been attacked!" he shouted, and raced ahead of the contingent behind him toward the inferno.

30

Deker jumped off his camel and raced down the hillside toward the new Israelite encampment, watching the columns of smoke rise into the setting sky, worried that the war for the Promised Land was over before it had even begun and that Israel's future and his own were lost forever.

His first hint that something was off was the Judean guards at the eastern edge of the camp. Unlike the Gadites back at Adam, they welcomed him not with shouts and arrows into the air but with bows trained on him until they saw Salmon, Achan, Elezar and the Gadites behind him with their banners.

"Has Hamas struck?" Deker asked.

"No," said a guard. "As soon as the Amorite kings west of the Jordan and all the Canaanite kings along the coast heard how Yahweh had dried up the Jordan before us until we crossed over, their hearts melted in fear and they no longer had the courage to back up Hamas and face us! Yahweh reigns!"

"Then what happened?" Deker demanded. "Where is the rest of the army?"

But the guards preferred instead to report everything to Salmon in clipped words Deker couldn't understand.

As Deker left them and marched ahead toward the camp, he saw no men, only women with baskets full of grain picked in the Promised Land. Some were dumping their grain into four silos freshly dug into the side of a small hill. On the hill were six distinctive redbud trees, their thick, bent trunks ablaze with pink flowers. Beyond the hill was the rest of the camp: tents, tarps, stables and the distant plumes of smoke and fire.

What the hell is going on? Deker wondered, and then he stopped in his tracks.

There before him, in the center of the camp, was the golden Ark of the Covenant, incandescent with the reflection of the surrounding fires, perched atop a pyramid of twelve tribal dolmen stones.

The sight of it took Deker's breath away.

He stumbled forward toward the altar of stone, both drawn toward the Ark and yet cautious to keep a safe distance. The Levites had erected a perimeter of poles with banners about twenty cubits around the altar, and here he stopped.

Elezar was right behind him, also breathless. "This is only a tenth the distance required when the Ark is in motion during battle. Enjoy the view now with your naked eyes, Deker, because I don't think we'll ever see it again in our lives."

Deker was mesmerized. The chest of shittimwood was smaller than Deker had imagined: not even two meters long, and barely a meter wide and tall. But its gold overlay gave it a jewel-like aura. A crown of gold cropped the top edges of the chest, on top of which stood two golden cherubs, their wings extended to form the mercy seat.

And on top of that mercy seat, according to Jewish tradition, sat the invisible presence of Yahweh.

"Inside this Ark are the tablets Moses smashed, the manna from heaven and the rod of Aaron with a flower bud," Elezar told him reverentially. "They represent the presence of God, the provision of God and the resurrection power of God."

But all Deker could think of was the shittim wood beneath the gold of the Ark, and that only made his mind go back to the death grove at Camp Shittim. Had that same horror been repeated here? Where were the soldiers?

He looked around and saw no bodies hanging from trees. But he saw no troops either. Only some commotion farther inside the camp that demanded attention.

31

Beyond the Ark stood the priest Phineas, recounting the crossing of the Jordan to several thousand children spread out as far as Deker's eyes could see, all the way to the mysterious, natural-gas–like bursts of fire at the south end of the camp.

"So when the people broke camp to cross the Jordan, the priests carrying the Ark of the Covenant went ahead of them!" Phineas cried out. "Now the Jordan is at flood stage all during harvest. Yet, as soon as the priests who carried the Ark reached the Jordan and their feet touched the water's edge, the water from upstream stopped flowing. It piled up in a heap a great distance away, at a town called Adam in the vicinity of Zarethan, while the water flowing down was completely cut off. So the priests who carried the Ark of the Covenant of the Lord stopped in the middle of the Jordan and stood on dry ground, while all Israel passed by until the whole nation had completed the crossing on dry ground."

Something like that, Deker thought, and wondered to what extent Phineas' revisionist history was what Salmon and Achan had heard as children about the parting of the Red Sea. Even the fate of the dolmen stones now under the Ark, which earlier had formed the stone bridge across the Jordan, got a poetic rendition.

"So the Israelites did as Joshua commanded them. They took twelve stones from the middle of the Jordan, according to the number of the tribes of the Israelites, as the Lord had told Joshua; and they carried them over with them to their camp, where they put them down. In the future, when your children ask you, 'What do these stones mean?' tell them that the flow of the Jordan was cut off before the Ark of the Covenant of the Lord. When it crossed the Jordan, the waters of the Jordan were cut off. These stones are to be a memorial to the people of Israel forever."

The altar of dolmen stones holding up the Ark was assembled like a ziggurat and stood about four meters tall—six dolmens across the bottom, four across the middle and two across the top. The altar was a stone monument unto itself, which was probably the intent as soon as the Ark was lifted up and out by the Levites to carry before the armies of Israel.

Deker looked at the dolmen stones and realized it must have taken a company of men from each tribe to haul each one out of the river and drag it to this place.

But it was all part of the show, and Deker could see Elezar take a seat on the ground in front of a couple of small children and nod his approval to an appreciative Phineas.

As he stared at the remarkable scene, he sensed somebody standing next to him. It was Salmon, who had gone from sullen to exultant.

"Bin-Nun has done it!" he said.

"Done what, Salmon?"

"Honored Yahweh by bringing us here forty years to the day of the Passover in Egypt before the Exodus. Tonight we celebrate the Passover in the Promised Land!"

"That was the hurry to cross the Jordan at flood stage?" Deker asked. "He wanted to hit a date?"

"This is his sign from Yahweh," Salmon said. "Don't you see? All of this is the sign the people needed to see."

"What sign do you see, Salmon? I see no sign."

"The holiness of Yahweh is before your eyes in the Ark."

Deker thought back again to his bar mitzvah, and the symbol of the Ark and how he had dropped the Torah. "You mean the 613 laws and purification rituals to show how ungodly we mortals are."

Salmon looked at him curiously. "The Torah and Law of Moses do not promise salvation, because keeping them all is impossible. The Law reflects the holiness of Yahweh, to show us our dependence on Yahweh's grace like Abraham. Without the Law we would know neither justice nor mercy."

Salmon sounded like Rahab up on her terrace in Jericho. True believers in a world ruled by those who seemed to make up the rules to suit themselves. It was beginning to make sense to Deker now, this notion that the fledgling nation of Israel existed to bear witness to the Law in a lawless world. But not this idea of faith in Yahweh's mercy. Thus far he had seen little of that from Bin-Nun.

"Bin-Nun has depended on nothing but me so far, Salmon. Phineas too."

"You will tonight," Salmon promised. "All the troops will."

"That's the problem, Salmon. I don't see any troops. Where are they?"

"Healing."

"Healing? From what?"

"Come with me and I'll show you."

32

Deker followed Salmon to the Tent of Meeting, where a line of Gadites snaked outside with Achan at the end. Salmon and Deker walked past them inside the tent where Deker saw General Bin-Nun in the front with a priest beside him at the altar. The troops were lined up as though they were about to receive Communion, but it was no cup that Bin-Nun held in his hand.

"It's a flint knife," Salmon explained from the back corner of the tent where they stood.

"I see the knife, Salmon. Who is the priest?"

"Phineas' father, Eleazer. His name is almost the same as the good angel."

The good angel.

Deker watched as a soldier dropped his field kilt and knelt before Bin-Nun, his back toward the line, and looked up at his leader. Bin-Nun fixed his gaze on his soldier and brought down his knife. Deker himself tensed at the sound of the blade scraping

the stone. There was a pause, and then Bin-Nun used his blade to
flick a piece of foreskin to a pile at the end of the altar.

"Holy God," he said under his breath. "He's circumcising
them, Salmon. But why? They're adults."

"Our fathers who came out of Egypt were circumcised,
but we who were born in the wilderness were not," Salmon
explained. "Today Yahweh has rolled away the reproach of
Egypt from us. The sons of Israel can finally take the place of
their fathers. That is why General Bin-Nun is calling this place
Gilgal."

A hot fury quickly succeeded Deker's revulsion. His efforts to
save Bin-Nun's army when they were most vulnerable, crossing
the Jordan in a single day, were all for naught. This stupid mutilation of the troops would set back the attack on Jericho by days if
not weeks. Rahab would remain at risk, and Hamas would have an
incalculable reprieve to regroup and draw help from neighboring
cities. Worse, it left the Israelite troops at less than half strength.
Hamas could attack them at any moment.

"This is insane," he said, trying to keep his voice low, but
aware that his raspy words and snarling tone had turned several
soldiers' heads. "You can't sack a city after you chop off the tips of
your men's dicks."

Salmon moved closer to Deker, trying to shield his anger
from the others. His eyes were still bright with hope, his voice
imploring. "But this is the sign of faith in Yahweh from Bin-
Nun we've been looking for," Salmon said. "Don't you see? Bin-
Nun has surrendered his war plans to Yahweh and seeks a new
directive. Yahweh will lead the way in battle now. Bin-Nun is

announcing it was Yahweh and not Moses who led us through the desert for forty years to test our hearts. And it will be by the hand of Yahweh and not the edges of our swords that we take the Promised Land."

Deker asked, "How long will the healing take?"

"They say about fourteen days for the healing to be complete," Salmon said. "But the men can fight after seven, which is the end of the Feast of Unleavened Bread, which begins tomorrow."

Seven days! Deker thought. Rahab could be dead by then. She could be dead already if Hamas suspected that she gave the Hebrew spies thc intel on his ambush plans. Meanwhile, they were all sitting ducks in this Gilgal place, with troops operating at less than half capacity.

What Bin-Nun was doing, Deker now concluded, was cleverly securing single-minded devotion from his troops ahead of the impending attack on Jericho. Circumcision and the Feast of Unleavened Bread during the healing would keep the men from feasting on sex with their wives and food from the new land. There would be no repeat of the mistake Moses had allowed when the Israelites first pitched camp at Shittim in Moab.

Deker knew then and there he had to grab the rest of his explosives from Kane and break for Jericho that very night. He had done Bin-Nun's dirty work twice now. He could wait no longer.

"I'm up soon," Salmon told him stoically. "You'll stay to watch?"

Watch? Deker knew Salmon considered this bizarre mutilation of male adults a holy ritual. But Deker had seen enough.

"I'll skip the butcher shop, Salmon. I'm already cut and ready for action."

As Deker left the tent, he sensed Bin-Nun's eyes follow him on his way out. But Deker didn't look back, only heard the sound of the flint knife strike the stone and the scrape of the blade behind him.

33

Waiting until it was completely dark and the Passover meals had begun in the tents throughout Gilgal, Deker quietly made his way to the dramatic fires at the south end of the camp facing Jericho. There he beheld acres and acres of smelting furnaces—hundreds of them—stoked by Kane the Kenite's army of metalsmiths. The pillars of fire lit up the night.

Bin-Nun has bred his army, Deker thought. Now he was going to forge his swords.

But as Deker looked closely at the smelting furnaces on his way to find Kane, he noticed only wood was going in to stoke the fires. Not a single blade or any other metal was being forged.

These pyrotechnics, he realized, were yet another example of Bin-Nun's psychological warfare designed to strike the fear of God into the melting hearts of the Reahns huddled behind their walls. He could only imagine how the multiplication of Israel's pillar of fire into more than three hundred fires looked to Rahab and what must be going through her mind even now.

At the same time, the firewall proved to be an invaluable defensive move, blocking the ability of the Reahn watchtowers to see behind it. Deker knew from night training how a bright object at night affected the naked eye's ability to see behind it. A Reahn on the walls who turned his eyes away from the fires might require a half hour for his eyes to readjust. Bin-Nun, meanwhile, could safely maneuver his troops behind the light until he was ready to attack. Deker supposed the same could be true in the daytime with the smoke. Either way, the Reahns were blind.

"Is anything around here real?" he asked when he saw Kane standing outside his tent, tending to one of his larger furnaces.

Kane was smoking some stinking, home-fashioned cigar and seemed to have been expecting him. "Only the tin and copper inside the treasury of Jericho."

Deker had already begun to suspect as much.

"So that explains why Bin-Nun is attacking Jericho," Deker said. "And why he's going to kill every breathing thing in Jericho, burn all its grain instead of feeding his own people with it and declare a *herem* ban preventing anyone from picking up even a penny from the blood-puddled streets under penalty of death. He says he needs the metals for the Treasury of Yahweh. But they're for you, Kane, so you can forge them into the weapons the Israelite war machine will need to fight in the wars beyond Jericho."

"The survival of Israel is at stake," Kane said, pushing his iron poker into the furnace to stoke the fire. "If we prevail against Jericho, we will need all the weapons we can forge if we are to have any hope of going up against the superior armies of the five kingdoms to the south and the even stronger armies to the north.

Gilgal here will serve as a station for the rest of the campaign for the Promised Land," he pointed out. "The troops can pass through anytime for repairs and new weapons."

"After they destroy Jericho and everyone inside."

"Every breathing thing," Kane said. "From the river to the Great Sea."

Deker stood in the glow of the heat and looked out across the desert toward Jericho. He couldn't even see it. All their lights were out, like a blackout for an air raid. Deker wouldn't be surprised if many Reahns, despite the assurances of General Hamas, feared hailstones of fire were about to rain down on them as they had on the Egyptians forty years ago. Such was the cloud of terror General Bin-Nun had successfully blown over their walls. But it was a mirage that would blow over soon enough, and the walls would still be standing when it did unless Deker took action.

"Give me my explosives," Deker demanded.

Kane eyed him up and down. Deker flashed no blade, but Kane seemed to understand Deker didn't need anything more than his bare hands to kill quickly and quietly. "You want to go to Jericho tonight?"

"We promised her," Deker said.

Kane screwed up his eyes. "Rahab the harlot?"

Deker nodded.

"Well, Israel must keep her word," Kane said. "But you don't need explosives to protect her. There's nothing you can do for her right now."

"I can bring down the walls."

"You'll do that when we attack."

"The attack is at least seven days away, Kane. Rahab and her family could be tortured and killed by then. Hamas must realize somebody told us about his plans to cut us off at the Jordan. And now that we've crossed, somebody is going to pay, and it's probably going to be her or those close to her. We might pass over her treason, but Hamas won't, and her blood will be on our hands."

Kane looked stern. "Bringing down the walls before we attack will only enable and encourage the Reahns to flee their city."

"Exactly," Deker said. "No genocide. I've seen the future, Kane. Israel will only make the world hate it by killing everything that breathes. I can change it."

"You believe that the nations will hate the Hebrews because of anything the Hebrews do or don't do?"

"Yes."

"They hated the Hebrews when they were slaves. They hate them now that they're warriors. Sparing Jericho won't change that. Neither can you."

"I can try."

"But if you succeed, the Reahns will take their treasure with them. We won't have enough weapons."

"Maybe if I succeed, Israel won't need as many."

Kane stood looking at Deker for a long moment. Deker couldn't tell if his eyes held pity or a kind of respect. Finally, Kane turned toward his tent and said, "I have something for you."

He left Deker at the furnace and disappeared behind the flap of his tent.

Deker looked around at the pillars of fire lined up across the desert. Bin-Nun had erected as much of a wall to keep the

Israelites inside Gilgal as he had to keep the Reahns out. And his circumcision of the troops guaranteed no desertions before the attack. Was Gilgad that different at this point than Jericho? Was General Bin-Nun truly as morally superior to General Hamas as Salmon insisted? Or was he only going to destroy a wall of stone in order to replace it with a wall of religion in the name of Yahweh?

Kane emerged a moment later with Deker's explosives pack and a small ceremonial washbowl painted red and black. He handed the bowl to Deker delicately.

"I kept one of your bricks and used it to make this."

Deker's hands trembled as he stared at the bowl. It looked just like the kind he had seen in Rahab's place, but the shape reminded him of another, more terrible piece of pottery that had claimed Rachel's life back in the Israel he knew.

"What's this for?" Deker said, fighting to keep his voice from shaking.

"To take with you inside the city when you go back," Kane told him. "Bin-Nun says you've proven yourself. Both with the intelligence about Hamas' plan to cut us down at the water, and by damming the Jordan at Adam. He never expected you to get this far. None of us did. Now only one thing remains: the walls."

Deker took the bowl, wrapped it in sackcloth and put it in his pack and counted fifteen C-4 bricks left from his original cache. It wasn't as much power as he wanted. He would have to be pinpoint accurate with where he laid the blasts and how he allocated the bricks between them. Assuming he got that far.

"God is my strength and power," Kane told him. "He teaches my hands to make war, so that my arms can bend a bow of bronze.

But I have not seen such a display of his power in anyone besides Moses—and you."

"What are you saying?" Deker asked.

"Even Moses did not set foot where we stand—east of the Jordan. Because he could not control the power God had granted him. Be careful, Deker. Once you set loose the power of God, even you cannot control it."

34

S am Deker flew like a phantom under the full moon, through the forests of palm trees, farmlands and abandoned hamlets. He wanted to save Rahab as much as Israel. But it was Rachel's death he remembered now as he ran toward Jericho.

It was Monday, March 29, 2010. Passover.

Deker sat in the café, sipped his coffee and stared through the window at the three-story yellow bungalow across the narrow street in East Jerusalem. He glanced at his new Krav Maga watch, a gift from Rachel. Ten minutes past six, which left him twenty-two minutes until sunset. Rachel was probably at the Western Wall by now, preparing her Shabbat candle for the first evening of Passover and herself for disappointment when he failed to show up for her yet again.

He patted the pocket of his dark kurta shirt and pulled out a small pen-shaped detonator with a red button at the end. A single tap would raise the trigger. A second tap would detonate the C-4 explosive disguised as a ceramic bowl inside the bungalow's second-floor parlor. He twisted the safety feature at the base of the pen to reset the trigger to prevent any premature accident and put it back in his pocket.

The bungalow was an elegant older building crammed between the newer multistory apartment buildings. It was also the home of Abdul Omekh, who had served as chief of staff to the former Palestinian Authority president, Mahmoud Abbas. These days Omekh was a professor of modern history at Al-Quds Open University and lectured that the Jews had no historical connection to Jerusalem or the Western Wall.

Tonight Omekh was hosting a special dinner of great interest to the IDF. Four cars already had pulled up and left within the past half hour, depositing guests. One of these guests, according to IDF intel, was the Black Dove, a Palestinian mole within Israel's counterterrorism unit whom no one had been able to unmask.

Deker was a demolitions specialist, not an assassin, and he had told his superiors that he thought this plan was a bad idea. Already he could imagine the lead in the *Jerusalem Post*: "A powerful bomb blast killed one of the Palestinian Authority's leading political scientists last evening in East Jerusalem as he sat down to dinner with family and friends." University students and colleagues would describe Omekh as "a respected professor." Hard-liners would describe him as "a revolutionary martyred by Israeli terrorists."

Deker instead suggested placing a camera in the bungalow to make the identification and deal with Black Dove at a time and place of the IDF's choosing. But his crazy new superior, Uri

Elezar, insisted it was better to take care of the Black Dove now and identify him later through dental records.

So last week Deker and his partner Stern paid a service call to the bungalow in a Gihon Water and Sewage Company van. The rains must have backed up the sorry sewers in the street again, the housekeeper explained, and now the stench was filling the home only days before an important dinner. When Stern returned to the van an hour later with a plumber's snake and planted a bag of clumpy drain blockage, he handed Deker the bowl from the table in Omekh's parlor.

It was the first time Deker held the original bowl in his hands, and he was pleased with how exact a replica he had made of it with his C-4 bowl based on photos Stern had snapped from his first service call a few days prior. So exact was his copy of this bowl that for a second he worried Stern had botched the switch. But then he saw a chip beneath the base of the bowl and got angry with Stern.

"Did you chip this bowl?" Deker demanded.

Stern looked doubtful. "I don't think so, boss."

Deker swore. "My bowl has no chip," he said, and started reviewing the photos of the bowl that Stern had snapped before. He couldn't see a chip. "What happens if Omekh sees that his bowl has magically repaired itself? He'll know it's been switched, and we won't get another shot at the Black Dove."

So far, however, it appeared that Omekh had noticed nothing. The GPS tracker in the bowl showed it was still in Omekh's parlor.

Now the last car pulled up and Deker saw one of the few

guests he could identify—a Hamas section chief—step out, followed by two more men Deker didn't recognize. They were patted down at the door by two plainclothes security types and then disappeared inside. The car drove off and Deker took out his monocular and looked up at the second-floor window. All the guests had gathered in the parlor. Everybody who was going to attend had arrived.

Deker glanced at his watch. It was 6:15 p.m.

The bronze sky outside the café seemed to weigh heavily over the squat buildings as sunset neared. But the narrow street was livelier than Deker had hoped. There were women carrying grocery bags, boys riding bicycles and street vendors hawking their wares. The explosion would shatter windows for fifty to one hundred meters around, and Deker worried about injuring innocents in the street.

Rachel, of course, would be mortified to know that this was why he had missed her at the Western Wall tonight. Nasty business, and he was through with it. Which was why he would never tell her, only ask her to marry him and move back to the States, where she could pursue her graduate degree in psychology and then spend the rest of her life rehabilitating him.

The thought of Rachel was the only thing that could bring a smile to his face. She knew something was up. She had come in on him at his apartment when he was hiding Omekh's chipped bowl in his closet. She must have suspected he had already picked up an engagement ring. She had made some passing remark at dinner a few days later about "conflict" or "blood" diamonds and how important it was to make sure you knew where things really came from, and not to support industries that exploited children or funded wars.

Fortunately, he would be able to assure her that the diamond he was giving her had come from his nana, and the only conflict it had seen was World War II. They could then talk about their bright, open future together. Deker yearned for that kind of innocence and passion for life again—before his two wars with the U.S. in Iraq and Afghanistan and this recent stint with the IDF in Israel.

Rachel was the way.

Deker looked at his watch. It was 6:16 p.m. He could picture her right now at the Western Wall. He could see her pour the water into a special bowl for the Shabbat hand-washing ceremony and dry her soft, strong hands with her little towel. And now, at exactly eighteen minutes to sunset, she was lighting her Shabbat candle.

As the candle burned, she would spread her hands around the flames and draw them inward in a circular motion three times to indicate the acceptance of the sanctity of Shabbat. Then she would cover her eyes and recite the blessing:

"Blessed are You, Lord our God, King of the Universe, who has hallowed us through His commandments, and has commanded us to kindle the lights of the holy Shabbat. Uncover your eyes and behold the Shabbat lights."

Deker swallowed and took the detonator out of his pocket again. He looked out the window of the café and pressed the red button twice and watched.

There was a terrific explosion, and he felt the café shake. But the villa across the street stood still. The explosion had come from several streets away.

People started shouting in the streets outside, but Deker just sat there, stunned.

Almost immediately the TV in the Arab café blared the news that a blast had gone off at the Western Wall. Two young men in back high-fived each other, but the half-dozen other faces watched in sober dismay.

Deker stared at the detonator in his hand as a wave of panic and nausea overwhelmed him.

No, no, no, he thought. *Jesus, no.*

Rachel.

35

Deker raced on foot through the twisting alleys of East Jerusalem toward the Temple Mount, tears forming in his eyes as he was breathing, "No, no, no!"

By the time he reached the Western Wall Plaza, the lights of the ambulances, police cars and news crews glowed in the twilight. He slowed his pace, catching his breath as he brushed past the EMTs toward the taped-off area.

Four people were dead, a newswoman was breathlessly reporting as she stared into the lens atop her cameraman's shoulder. Six others were injured, two critically.

He scanned the crowd as he pushed his way to the police line. There were more onlookers than people praying at the wall. Knowing Rachel, she'd be the first to be offering comfort to the victims or support to the first responders.

But he couldn't see her anywhere in the chaos.

He could, however, see Stern and Elezar standing to the side with a couple of plainclothes Mossad officers conducting their inspection before any evidence was completely contaminated. They were blocking his view.

He approached them slowly, not certain if he wanted to talk to them or not. His feet felt like lead, his mouth was dry. The shouts and cries circling his head from the crowd gave him a headache, and the sight of the small ceramic shard in Stern's hand made him nauseous.

It's the explosive bowl I made to blow up the Hamas gathering. I mixed it up with the original bowl. Rachel must have found it at home. Oh, my God. I've made a tragic mistake.

Their faces said everything when they half-turned and saw him. They looked away as he pushed his way through and beheld the charred bits of limbs and flesh of the victims strewn across the plaza.

Deker collapsed to his knees, his soul swallowed up by a black void of grief and hopelessness, and wailed like a dying animal.

Rachel was gone, and with her the spark of his own life.

36

Even from the abandoned farm, Deker could see from a distance that Jericho was sealed up tight as a drum. Everyone must have fled the surrounding fields as soon as the Israelites had crossed the Jordan and sought refuge inside the walls of the city. No one went in and no one came out.

That included Rahab, assuming she was still alive.

As he looked up to see the clouds move like a spirit across the moon and listened to the rustling trees whisper ancient secrets, Deker felt as if he were the last soul alive in this world.

Until he spotted a movement out of the corner of his eye.

Moving quickly and quietly through a date grove, careful not to betray himself with a sound, he peered out through some palm leaves and started.

Kneeling in the dirt, hands stretched out toward the heavens with his sword across them, was none other than General Joshua bin-Nun.

He seemed to be talking to somebody Deker couldn't see.

Deker squinted his eyes and scanned the horizon, looking for a security detail of young Judeans like Salmon and Achan—or, worse, Hamas and a squad of Reahn assassins. But there was nobody else.

Deker couldn't believe Bin-Nun would expose himself to the enemy while his troops were recovering from the mutilation he had inflicted on them back in Gilgal.

Deker whipped out his scythe sword, just in case he had missed some shadow force, and rushed through the brush toward Bin-Nun.

Bin-Nun, sensing his approach, spun around quickly with the point of his sword to Deker's throat, stopping him cold. Then, looking at him quizzically, Bin-Nun asked him, "You mean to save her, don't you?"

"I do." Deker sheathed his sword. "Who was that you were talking to? Why is the general out alone without his guards?"

"I came to inspect Jericho for myself," Bin-Nun told him. "I was praying and looked up and saw an angel standing in front of me with a drawn sword in his hand. It was a real angel, not like you. I went up to him and asked, 'Are you for us or for our enemies?' The angel replied, 'Neither, but as commander of the army of the Lord I have now come.'"

Deker took a breath. "The commander of the army of the Lord?" he repeated in as even a tone as possible, so as not to suggest he doubted Bin-Nun. "What did he say?"

Deker stiffened as Bin-Nun put a hand on his shoulder and turned him toward the city about a kilometer away. "Can you pick out this harlot's window in the city wall from here?"

Deker pointed. "That one: sixth window to the right along the north wall."

Bin-Nun asked, "You are certain?"

"Yes," Deker replied, although he wasn't really.

Bin-Nun glanced at the pack of explosives Deker had slung over his shoulder. "You will enter the city through the harlot Rahab's window tonight with your explosives," he told him, and Deker felt a wave of electricity rise up his spine as the words he longed to hear spilled from Bin-Nun's lips. "You will lie in wait for six days, and on the seventh day you will blow the walls on our signal. This is the plan that Yahweh has revealed to Israel."

Deker nodded. He hadn't seen this angel of the Lord, but he was pleased with the angel's instructions to Bin-Nun all the same, as well as Bin-Nun's response of faith in going along with them. Surely that would make the Levites happy. "How will I know the signal?"

"For six days the army will march around Jericho behind the Ark of the Covenant and seven priests carrying rams' horns," Bin-Nun said. "But on the seventh day we'll circle the walls seven times with the priests blowing their trumpets. Listen for a long blast on the trumpets. That's when I'll have the army give the war cry. Our shout will be your signal to blow the walls. We'll rush the stairway of rubble you will have created and climb over the walls and into the city. The city will be doomed to destruction and all who are in it."

Even as Bin-Nun spoke these final words, Deker could hear footsteps in the brush growing louder and turned to see Elezar emerge from the shadows, eyes on fire.

"General Bin-Nun," Elezar said, breathing hard as he glared at Deker. "What is the meaning of this?"

Deker cleared his throat. "We are discussing Rahab the harlot and her family," he said quickly. "She hid us from Hamas and helped us escape with the knowledge of his plans to cut us down at the Jordan. She also warned us to march at least five hundred cubits away from the walls to remain outside the long range of the archers."

Bin-Nun pursed his lips. Deker had forgotten to give him that intel earlier about the kill zone, and it was clear the general considered it more than useful. Then again, Deker spared Bin-Nun the obvious reminder that he himself had made a similar sort of promise to Rahab's grandmother forty years ago, and that it was about time he fulfilled it.

"Rahab the harlot shall be spared," Bin-Nun said, and Deker felt his lungs exhale in relief. "Only Rahab and all who are with her in the house, because she hid you, and only on two conditions."

Deker took a breath and waited. So did Elezar, keenly searching for any loopholes Bin-Nun might give him.

"First, you will make sure she binds a scarlet cord in the window through which she let you down and which you are about to climb up," Bin-Nun said. "This will be a sign to me that she hasn't betrayed you to Hamas. It will also be a sign for our troops to avoid her house when we storm the city walls. If she fails to do this, we will be blameless in her death."

Deker nodded. This was the very blood-on-the-doorposts Passover protection and sign of her faith in Yahweh that Rahab had been seeking all along.

Deker asked, "And the second condition?"

"She must bring her entire family into her house, or they will be slaughtered with the rest of the Reahns," Bin-Nun stated. "Whoever ventures outside the doors of her house into the street, his blood—or hers—shall be on his own head, and we will be guiltless. If any of our men lay a hand on her family inside her house, their blood will be on our head."

It was Deker's turn to glare at Elezar. "Got that?" he said, and turned his face to the walls of Jericho.

37

Deker could see the walls clearly as he and Elezar approached slowly and quietly in their camouflaged uniforms they had soiled with the dirt in which they now crawled. The concrete revetment wall ahead cut an even line across the sandy ground, the jagged brick wall above it rising into the dark. Every now and then, when a cloud broke to reveal a thin shaft of moonlight, he could glimpse the Reahn helmets and spears waiting for them atop the wall.

According to his calculations, Rahab's cellar window on the north wall was only thirty or so meters from the main gate around the corner at the east wall. So Deker used the gatehouse tower to his left and the forbidding city spire dead ahead as his markers all the way in. But the walls were coming up fast now, blocking his view of the markers, and the clouds were parting too much, forcing him and Elezar to move more quickly than they'd like to keep from being spotted overhead.

Deker dragged himself across the sand to the base of the wall when a dazzling white light from the sky stabbed the ground just behind him and in front of Elezar, who stopped cold just outside the patch of light.

Deker pressed his back against the rock and held his breath in the shadows. The ground was awash with moonlight now, brought by a break in the night clouds. Deker was aware of the crunch of boots and the sound of voices growing louder on the wall high above.

"Clear!" shouted one of the Reahn sentries.

"All clear!" repeated another sentry.

Soon Deker was standing up, back flat against the wall, staring out toward Gilgal and its awesome pillars of fire, waiting for Elezar. For a terrifying moment, Elezar looked as though he were sure he had been spotted and was about to do something stupid. But the shaft was cut off again by another cloud and Elezar made it over quickly in the dark.

"They can't see a damn thing with the fires, Elezar," Deker assured him in a low whisper. "We just have to keep quiet."

Deker turned and looked up the sheer face of the wall. There beyond his view was Rahab's window. All he needed to do was climb the wall, pull himself through the window in Rahab's cellar and then drop Elezar a rope. The reddish brick wall that began five meters overhead was uneven enough that an experienced climber like himself could manage it without much difficulty.

It was the first five meters—that damn concrete revetment wall—that was the problem. Deker dropped his pack, pulled off his boots and tied them to his belt. Then he picked up the axe inside his sack that Kane had packed.

"I need to stand on your shoulders," Deker told Elezar, who nodded as he breathed harder and louder than Deker would have preferred.

Elezar bent over and Deker climbed onto his back until he stood on his shoulders.

The top of the revetment wall formed a tiny ledge at the base of the brick wall above. It was just out of his reach.

Deker slid his hand behind his back to his belt and pulled out the axe. He raised it as high as he could, his feet shifting as Elezar moved beneath him, and hooked the axe head on the ledge. It held sufficiently for him to pull himself high enough to grab the ledge with his other hand.

He could feel Elezar fall away from him. He then dropped the axe and grabbed the ledge with both hands, swinging one foot up. With three points of contact he was able to pull his entire body up, belly flat against the wall, arms spread wide.

Deker caught his breath and slowly made his way up the wall, digging his fingers and toes into any solid crevice he could find. Some crevices were more solid than others, and at one point halfway up a brick gave way and he lost his footing, leaving him hanging by two fingers. He looked down to see the broken pieces crash to the ground, where there was no sign of Elezar.

The sound of the falling brick must have alerted the sentries overhead, because he could see a couple of torches above him.

"They just reinforced that section last season," said a Reahn sentry, from what Deker could gather.

"I'm not reporting it" was the reply of a second sentry. "Hamas might make me go out and fix it."

A third sentry laughed. "Afraid some Hebrew is going to reach up from the shadows and grab you by the ankles and drag you down to hell?"

It was a thought. But Deker was too far down the wall for that, and still hanging by his two fingertips while his foot searched for a toehold. With immense relief he found one a moment later. Once he was sure the sentries were gone, he continued to work his way up the ragged brick wall until he could see the shape of an open square window above him.

He paused, sweat dripping into his eyes, and realized that he could be wrong about this window, despite what he had told Bin-Nun. It might not be the same window that Rahab had lowered him out of.

Lord, help me, he prayed, knowing full well that he had already committed himself at this point to entering this window. Before Deker had even thought to pray, the good Lord would have had to rearrange the entire architecture of Jericho to suddenly make this Rahab's window if he was wrong. Which seemed ludicrous to Deker. *I'll never have the faith of Abraham.*

Cautiously, he raised himself up so he could look inside. But it was too dark to make out anything. He listened for a moment. Then, detecting no sound, he crawled through the window and into the cellar hewn out of the city wall.

With immense relief he realized that this was, indeed, Rahab's cellar. He took a breath, said a silent prayer of thanks and began to look for the rope that Rahab had used to let them down before so he could help Elezar up.

He found the rope coiled in a corner among the jars and skeletons.

He never thought he'd be so happy to see those Reahn skeletons again. He picked up the rope and turned toward the window to let it down for Elezar.

But as he moved toward the square of stars, a big shadow moved in front of the window. A feeling of blind panic seized Deker as all the skeletons in the room seemed to step toward him.

Then the grillwork behind him opened and he saw a hooded figure holding an oil lamp. The hood came down and he saw Rahab, dressed much more modestly than during their first encounter.

"Rahab," he said, starting toward her.

But she said nothing, looking over his shoulder.

Her oil lamp flickered and Deker looked around the dimly illuminated cellar. He was surrounded by four Reahn soldiers.

They must have been waiting for me as soon as they saw the pillars of fire go up at Gilgal and knew the Israelites had crossed the Jordan.

Rahab pointed at him and told the soldiers, "This is the Hebrew spy."

38

Deker watched Elezar haul himself through the window. He looked relieved to set his feet on solid ground until he saw the four Reahn soldiers behind Deker.

"Rahab's brothers," Deker told him. "We're good."

Rahab said, "They were all conscripted into the Reahn army as teens. Their uniforms disguise their hearts. We aren't all what we seem."

With a steely gaze Elezar asked, "How is this good, Deker?"

"They're going to get me into the fortress to plant the C-4," Deker said. "They know the weak spots in the wall. I'm going to plant two charges with timers—one short and one long—to blow the walls. Fortress wall first, city wall second."

Rahab translated what Deker was saying to the biggest and apparently the oldest of her brothers, who looked no older than twenty-four and whose rippling physique would have qualified him as a Mr. Universe contestant in the twenty-first century.

Ram, as Rahab called her older brother, looked at him

intensely, with all the passion of an eldest brother. His unspoken warning seemed to say, *Mess with my sister and I'll rip your head off.* Then he turned to Rahab and said something in a deep, gruff voice.

Rahab said, "Ram knows the disbursement of troops in the city, the checkpoints and roadblocks, as well as the layout of the fortress, secret gates and guard shifts. But he wants to know what assurances we have, if we help you now, that your soldiers won't destroy us along with Reah?"

Deker glanced at Elezar and in English said, "Nice to know that at least they think I'll be successful."

"Tell her we gave her our word and that's enough," Elezar replied, going back to his original non-promise to her when she first helped them escape a week earlier.

"Thank God even Bin-Nun is more principled than you." Deker shook his head and turned to Rahab and said, "General Bin-Nun declares that you and all who are with you in your house will be spared on two conditions."

Rahab repeated this to Ram, who showed no change in expression, and looked at Deker eagerly with her dark, animated eyes. "Tell us these conditions and we will meet them."

"I will meet one of them for you now."

Deker was aware of Elezar's death stare as he pulled out his dagger, cut a piece of the red rope on the floor and moved to the open window. He found one of the bronze hooks inside the top of the window used to keep grillwork in place. He fastened the scarlet cord to the hook and then closed the hook with one sharp, soft blow from his axe.

Now Bin-Nun and his scouts would know from the start that she hadn't betrayed him and everything was a go.

"This is your blood on your doorpost, Rahab," he told her. "This is the sign for our angels of death to pass over your house when they storm the city."

Deker watched her eyes grow wide and mouth drop as she heaved a sigh of relief and wonder. Truly, she considered this an answered prayer.

"If this cord should be removed, however," he warned her, "we will be blameless in your deaths."

Rahab nodded profusely and repeated everything to her brothers, who glanced at one another and nodded tentatively.

"What is the second condition?" she demanded anxiously.

"You must bring your entire family into this house or they will not be passed over and will be slaughtered with the rest of your people."

"You mean my mother and father and brothers?"

"Yes," he told her. "They will be spared."

"What about my brother Ram's family?"

Deker could hear Elezar groan behind him as he answered, "Them too."

"And my girls who work for me?"

"Holy shit," Elezar said. "Enough, Deker. One whore is enough."

Deker ignored him. "All who belong to you, Rahab," he said. "Bring them into your house. But do not tell them about our deal. Simply offer them refuge in advance of the siege."

Rahab again repeated everything to her brothers, who finally began to ease up. Deker realized she had probably negotiated quite a lot on behalf of the family for years and they'd trusted her on more than one occasion to secure the best terms on the deal points.

"Remember," Deker warned her again, "whoever ventures outside the door of your house into the street, his blood—or hers—shall be on his own head, and we will be guiltless."

Rahab nodded slowly, and Deker realized the deal had hit a snag.

"Here we go," grumbled Elezar.

"We have a problem," Rahab said. "Ram can get his family inside the house before the attack. But he must take his post on the walls when called or he will be labeled a deserter and they will look for him and his family."

"Then what's he doing here right now?" Elezar shot back.

"His shift starts soon," Rahab said. "He'll have to leave."

Elezar was suspicious. "How convenient that all of your brothers happen to be off duty just when we happen to climb through your window."

"Oh, these aren't all my brothers," Rahab said. "I have six more on duty right now."

"Jesus Christ, Deker!" Elezar cried out too loudly. "This is why Bin-Nun takes no prisoners."

The tension was palpable in the room, Rahab and her brothers listening carefully to see if Elezar's bark had attracted any attention, however unlikely that would be from their location.

Deker lowered his voice and said, "You want us to be captured, Elezar?"

"We're all but captured already, Deker, what with you bringing half the city into our little operation."

"That's why Ram here is taking me into the fortress tonight," Deker told them all.

Rahab gasped. "Bin-Nun is attacking tonight?"

"No. I am. With these."

Deker pulled out his C-4 bricks.

Rahab and her brothers looked completely mystified.

"Go ahead, Deker," Elezar goaded. "Explain your magic mud bricks to her. See what big Ram thinks of staking his life on something you can't demonstrate to him until you actually bring the walls down."

"These bricks create fire to melt your walls," he told them all, neglecting to mention that such a feat normally required hundreds of small shots and far more than six days to prep, and that was with robust computer technology to control and time the blasts to the millisecond.

Rahab translated.

"How can this be?" Ram demanded. "You have only fifteen bricks and our walls contain thousands upon thousands."

"I only have to melt a section of a wall, not the whole wall," Deker explained. "It's like cutting down a palm tree to make it fall in a particular direction. If you can help me find the weakest part of the northern wall of the fortress, I can melt the bricks at the bottom. All the bricks on top of it will collapse and avalanche down the slope and maybe break through the lower city."

"So what you're really saying is that you're going to blow the walls tonight if you can," Elezar said, challenging him before Rahab and her brothers.

Deker said, "If Reahn security proves tougher than expected

and forces me to plant one well-placed blast to bring down both walls at once, then yes, I have to take the shot."

"That's not the plan," Elezar said, careful not to tip off the six-day timetable to Rahab and her brothers.

"And Bin-Nun told you this when?" Deker asked. "I recall you missing the first half of my conversation with him out in the fields."

"It's in the bloody Hebrew Bible, you ignoramus. But I forgot. You don't read."

Elezar was standing by the window for effect, the pillars of fire in the distance, the threat of Yahweh's coming wrath palpable to Rahab and her brothers.

All Deker could think of right now was the bowl in his pack that Kane had given him, and the memory of how he had failed to save Rachel. He wouldn't fail Rahab.

Deker lowered his voice and spoke in English. "The longer we wait, the more we risk exposure and capture by Hamas," he reasoned. "It's use them or lose them with the C-4 bricks."

"That's not your reason, Deker. You want to blow the walls so that Rahab and all the Reahns can escape. Once they see their defenses fall, they're going to run. That's not Bin-Nun's plan."

"Bin-Nun's plan is to murder every man, woman, child and animal." Deker looked at Rahab and said, "Plans change, Elezar. You said so yourself."

Elezar spat on the ground and straightened up by the window. "What are you doing, Commander?" he demanded of him in English, pulling rank on him.

"The Israelites are talking more than holy war . . . Colonel,"

Deker said, without the respect he knew his superior officer demanded. "They're talking genocide as a strategy to strike the fear of God into their enemies. To do that, they'll kill everything that breathes."

"So you think that if you blow the walls now, you'll put the fear of God not just into the Reahns but all the cities of Canaan."

"They'll surrender like Japan did after the Americans dropped the atom bomb, and Israel will have her Promised Land without the genocide," Deker explained. "Maybe this will generate some kind of good karma in the future and spare our people centuries of worldwide hatred and even the Holocaust you want to prevent."

"Maybe even save Rachel in the future?" Elezar added.

Deker nodded. That was exactly what he was hoping for. "Think, Elezar: we can stop the forever war between Jews and Arabs and the rest of the world."

"You're a fool, Deker. Your arrogance might not only get us killed here in this time, but it could also prevent us from even being born in the future, maybe even prevent the birth of Israel as a nation. You're the genocidal maniac, Deker, not Bin-Nun. Stand down."

Deker knew there was nothing Elezar could do to stop him now, so he ignored him and turned to Rahab. "So what now?" he asked in Hebrew.

"Ram will take you inside the fortress to set your signal," she told him, and looked over his soiled clothing. "Where is your uniform?"

"We left them behind to avoid detection when we approached the walls."

She matched him up with one of the other brothers, Rah, and they stripped and switched. Rah then gave him his identification card, a square of bronze with an official seal on it along with his engraved serial number: 3,257.

Deker showed Elezar the card and then looked at Rah: "You are number 3,257?"

Rahab translated and Deker suddenly seemed to understand the gist of their language when Rah spoke.

"I am," said Rah, with a *What's it to you?* inflection in his voice.

"Then there are at least 3,257 soldiers in Reah?"

"Ten thousand," Ram answered.

"Ten thousand?" Deker repeated to make sure he understood correctly, too easily expressing his surprise and spooking Rahab, Ram, Rah and the rest in the cellar. Then, aware of the stares, he got ahold of himself and took a breath. "The shadow army, of course."

Hamas had certainly evened his odds with Bin-Nun's 8,000 troops. No, he had done more than that. Suddenly the prospect of blowing the walls wasn't enough. Not if Bin-Nun was expecting to confront 1,500 Reahn troops inside the city, only to be swarmed by 10,000. How could he have missed the count so badly on his first visit? Where had Hamas hidden them?

"What's wrong?" Rahab asked him, and Deker could see her concern, but there was also a flicker of shame in her eyes that confused him.

"Nothing," Deker said, and strapped on his explosives pack. "I'd like to see this shadow army with my own eyes."

Ram nodded. "I'll take you now."

"Deker," Elezar said sternly. "We're supposed to wait."

"You wait here," Deker said, and gave Elezar five C-4 bricks and detonators and kept ten for the fortress wall.

Elezar seemed surprised that he would entrust him with the explosives. But Deker knew that if he succeeded in bringing down the upper fortress wall, these bricks weren't necessary. Faced with such a breach, the Reahns would surely pour out the main gate and flee. If he failed at the upper wall, he'd at least have some backup below. And if he was captured, the Reahns wouldn't have the remaining explosives.

"Once I've set the charges at the fortress and established the direction of destruction, I'll come back and we'll set the rest here farther north along the city wall that lines up with the first blast," he concluded. "Then we'll blow this whole thing open. Tonight if we can, later if we must."

39

Deker followed Ram past the blocks of darkened houses toward the fortress, smelling only suspicion and fear on the surface streets of Jericho. The citizens were holed up inside with their families, while the soldiers outdoors floated like shadows on the dim walls above and in the empty squares below.

In almost no time Deker followed Ram straight through the fortress gate. Not one guard dared stop the big Reahn and what appeared to be one of his many brothers nipping at his heels—such was Ram's reputation—and Deker began to appreciate even more the tangled web Rahab had spun just to make it this far to save her family.

Deker's plan to bring down the fortress involved setting off a blast in a weak spot in the northern wall, and this was where Ram said he would take them before they left Rahab's cellar. Deker had pointed him in the right direction by suggesting they find a section of the wall where a gate once existed but had since been walled up. Ram said he knew of just such a section.

Now the spire of Jericho's giant stone tower gleamed like a minaret against the full moon as they crossed the fortress's plaza. The iron door Ram was heading toward was on the opposite end of the plaza, in the middle of the north wall.

The central plaza of the fortress was dark, but Deker could make out the columns of the royal palace to his left and the colossal metallic temple of Molech glinting to his right. It was at least several stories tall, with two great bronze doors in its belly and a head in the shape of a bull.

Deker could almost feel Molech's eyes follow him and Ram toward the inside gate of the north wall.

So far, Deker had yet to see the garrison headquarters and troop barracks, let alone the military supply dumps. Which was odd, considering the number of troops Ram claimed Hamas had under his command.

The guards on duty at the iron gate recognized Ram and let them in.

What Deker found inside was another world: a network of tunnels built inside the fortress walls, floor upon floor.

"Welcome to our barracks," Ram said as they pushed their way through the crowded tunnels, past stepladders and rows of hammocks. Torches hung like chandeliers above to give as much shoulder room as possible.

This was how you hid ten thousand healthy, well-fed troops in a city of two thousand or so, Deker thought: pack them inside the upper walls enclosing the six-acre summit of Jericho's inner fortress.

"The shadow army?" Deker asked quietly.

"Yes," Ram grunted.

"So there are at least as many more in the lower city wall?" Deker pressed, knowing that perimeter wall around the entire eight-acre city mound could theoretically hold almost twice as many troops.

"We do not speak of those," Ram whispered gruffly.

At least, that's what Deker thought he said. "What do you mean?"

Ram either didn't understand him or was simply changing the subject. "The torches make it too bright in here. You are no longer my brother but a soldier. I don't know you. Follow me at intervals."

They crossed several more compartments and made their way past one of the mess halls before turning down a narrow flight of steps.

Deker could only marvel. This was a city within a city.

Although the tunnels in the wall were laid out in relatively straight lines, he quickly lost his sense of direction as he followed his guide up and down ladders and steps through various levels and compartments toward the middle of the north wall.

Their odyssey ended in a ghostly hall with a vaulted ceiling. The rotting wooden beams could barely support the caved-in roof, so a giant concrete pillar had been built to hold up the ramparts above.

And next to the pillar was the walled-up gate, its bricks a shade different from the rest of the interior wall.

But there was a problem. A lone stonemason stood before them in a dirty apron, wiping the grease from his hands with a blackened cloth. He wore a handkerchief knotted over his head, his angry eyes in his soot-smeared face looking Deker over.

"This is my relief?" he asked Ram.

"No. *This* is," Ram said, and snapped the mason's neck.

Deker watched the mason crumple to the floor and stared at Ram. "What did you do that for?"

Ram said, "He's going to die anyway, isn't he? Either by your mud bricks or by Bin-Nun's sword."

Deker couldn't really argue with that logic and didn't have the time. The clock was ticking and he had to get to work.

Thanks to Ram, he had located the critical structural element in the north wall. It wasn't the walled gate, as he had expected, but the concrete pillar. It was an impressive meter wide in diameter and ten meters tall.

"The mud bricks will remove this pillar, and removing this pillar will allow the rest of the wall to collapse on itself," Deker tried to explain to Ram as he set out his C-4 bricks. "Just like a tree falling down."

Ram looked up at the pillar thoughtfully and frowned. "But if you do that, then it will fall on top of the houses in the city below."

Deker said nothing, but he could see the reality sinking in as Ram had pictured it. Deker hoped Ram didn't have any relatives there. But from the size of Rahab's extended family, that seemed unlikely.

"What about the walled gate?" Ram asked. "That part of the wall seems weaker."

"This is better," Deker said. "I can't explain it now."

He could definitely blow open the walled gate. The blast would turn the bottom five meters of the fortress wall to rubble. The problem was at the top of the wall. The ramparts above were reinforced like a bridge for the troops to march between watch-towers. Deker would need to blow up the top several meters of the wall to get it to fall properly. Otherwise the rubble would block the Israelites from entering the fortress.

The key was this pillar. A single shot down the center would take it out.

He didn't need all ten bricks to take out this pillar and its section of the wall. But he had only one shot, and it would be messy. Ordinarily he'd use hundreds of small shots and control their timing with a handheld computer. Also, he'd usually have several days to prep this kind of blast. Now, however, he was trying to do it in less than an hour.

The big slowdown was loading the C-4 properly into the bottom of the pillar. Normally, he'd drill a few hundred holes for his explosives, each one less than two centimeters in diameter and a few centimeters deep. Tonight he was basically slapping bricks to a pillar, and had to take his time to place them properly.

He had one chance.

Deker worked quietly the next few minutes until he realized things were too quiet. Too late, he knew something was wrong and turned to see Ram holding a dagger.

"You!" Ram shouted, as if he'd never seen him before. "Spread your feet! Hands against the wall!"

Deker did as he was told and could feel the rough hands run over his body. "What are you doing?"

Ram spun him around and pushed the edge of his dagger under Deker's chin. "Say nothing," he said, his face close to Deker's, breathing heavily. "Nothing."

Ram must have heard something, because several torches bobbed up and down in the darkness and a deep voice boomed, "Ram, is that you?"

Deker remembered the voice from Rahab's terrace.

Hamas.

"Look what I found!" Ram said, and kicked Deker in the groin.

The blow sent Deker doubling over in agony. He slid against the wall to the floor, groaning in pain.

Ram then reached down and pulled him up by the hair. "You're in the hands of the Reahn National Guards now, Hebrew."

In spite of his jarring pain, Deker managed to stand up on his feet.

"Excellent work, Captain Ram," said Hamas, and Deker felt his eyes look him up and down, registering that the general was unimpressed with this Hebrew specimen. "Although I must say I was expecting a bit more coming from Bin-Nun."

Deker stared as Hamas walked toward him with several guards behind him, mouth in a snarl.

"I see you've killed one of my men, Hebrew." Hamas smiled. "When I'm done with you, you'll wish you were as fortunate."

A giant forearm swung out of nowhere across Deker's face, and everything went black.

40

There was a flash of light, and Deker felt another blow to his head. He opened his eyes in time to see Ram pull back his iron-hard fist and then bludgeon him in the face again.

"The invasion plans, Deker," said another voice with a thick Aramaic accent. "That's your name, Hebrew, isn't it?"

Deker blinked to see that he was in some dank cell, and that a large figure was standing next to Ram. The figure bent over, and his smooth face with hooded eyes and long hair came into focus.

Hamas. I've been captured. Maybe Ram has taken the credit.

A hand reached out toward the silver Star of David hanging around Deker's neck and roughly dangled it before his eyes. The IDF insignia in the center came in and out of focus, and Deker felt a profound aura of déjà vu settle over him.

"The Hebrew invasion plans," Hamas repeated. "Or Ram will have to kill you."

Deker spit in Ram's face, just to show Hamas they were on

different sides and to let Ram know that he needn't fear exposure—yet. Everything depended on how this all played out.

"What invasion?" Deker asked as Ram wiped the spit from his
face.

Hamas said, "Ram, show him."

Ram grabbed him by his hair and dragged him across the
floor with his chains and propped him up by the window. Deker
looked out to see a cloud of dust in the distance. There was the
glint of the golden Ark, seven priests with their trumpets in front
of it. Armed guards marched before the priests and behind the
Ark. They formed the clasp of a great necklace of Israelite soldiers encircling the city, six men deep and more than five hundred
cubits away beyond the range of the archers.

"That invasion," Hamas said as he stood behind him, and
Deker could smell his foul breath. "Behold the dust kicked up by
the vast host of Israelite troops. Bin-Nun has been circling the city
for six days now. Did you really think you could frighten us into
surrendering with tall tales of Yahweh's divine power?"

Deker tried to piece together how long he had been held
in captivity here. Surely it couldn't have been six days. But his
mind was a jumble of beatings and blackouts, and he had no clue.
He turned to look the general in the eye. "Whether I live or die,
Hamas, you already know that Bin-Nun is going to win no matter
what."

Hamas smiled. "It's been six days, Deker. Without you, they
have already failed. Including your comrade Elezar. He only lasted
two days before he died."

Elezar dead? Deker didn't believe it. Dogs like Elezar never died; they always survived somehow. That the Israelites were circling the city, however, was no lie. He could see it with his own eyes.

The familiar feeling of dread that so often overwhelmed him returned with a bitter vengeance. Deker cursed himself for his failure and resolved that, whatever else happened, he wouldn't break.

"Your cause is lost, Hamas."

"It's Bin-Nun who looks lost to me, Deker," Hamas said. "Is he waiting for a signal from you? Is that why he circles without striking? Or are you the one waiting for a signal from him?"

Deker said nothing.

"Ram, give him a signal."

Deker turned in time to see Ram cock his giant clenched fist before it hit him like a sledgehammer in the face. His head slammed against the wall and he blacked out.

41

Slowly the lights went on in Deker's head. He was in a small, spare room with a table and two chairs on either side. On the table were his bricks of C-4 and detonators and a bowl of rotten apples. Two guards stood at the door.

"I've always been fascinated by the occultic practices of the Hebrews, and before he died your comrade Elezar called these magic mud bricks," Hamas said. "What did he mean by that?"

Deker said, "If that's why you're keeping me alive, you're wasting your time, Hamas. Kill me and be done with it."

"I need you for the show trial. But you need not worry. It will be brief. And then you'll be exterminated. The people have to see that we're doing something about the Hebrew vermin crawling inside our walls."

Deker said nothing. He was too tired. Hamas was disappointed he hadn't gotten a rise out of him.

Hamas was smarter than he looked. But perhaps that was because of the care he took to maximize his size and build with his armor. He was beefier than the lean Israelite commanders. But his eyes betrayed a stormy disposition, as if he were constantly running scenarios through his head. None of the faraway look of a nut job like Bin-Nun. Perhaps because the Israelites had nothing to lose except their lives. Hamas was compromised in this way, dealing with fanatics like Bin-Nun and presumably Elezar. Perhaps he saw some hope in Deker—a kindred spirit, so to speak.

"Did you know Bin-Nun was a mercenary with the Egyptian army before the Exodus, Deker?" Hamas said. "Oh, yes. He and my father served together. They even got cut together. That's right. Circumcision used to be a rite of passage for elite Egyptian officers. I see that Bin-Nun has begun to institute the practice with his men, like you. What I can't understand is why he'd risk using such men as spies. It's a dead giveaway that you're a Hebrew. Because you're certainly no Egyptian."

Deker was clothed now, but Hamas had wanted him to know he had been carefully inspected.

"You know what I do with my men who disappoint me?" Hamas asked rhetorically as he picked up a worm-ridden apple from the bowl of fruit and began to slice it and the worms to pieces. "I cut off their penises and then their balls to make them eunuchs so they can become priests in the service of Molech. It's a shame I can't do the same to you. But I need to show your circumcision at the trial to prove you're Hebrew. No matter. It's not like you'll ever get to use it with Rahab again." Hamas paused for effect. "I'd hate to drag her into this nasty business."

Deker showed no emotion, but Hamas smiled as he stood up

and pointed his knife over the table at him. The Reahn general either suspected or knew for certain that Deker was one of the two spies who had escaped him the week before at Rahab's.

"You think you can drop into my city for a night and make one of our moon princesses fall in love with you and risk her life and family for a bunch of Hebrews? Which is more likely, Deker: that Rahab used me to pass along information of our fortifications to you, or that she used you to betray your invasion plans?"

Deker stared at the mud bricks spread out before him as evidence. "I don't believe you."

"Just explain the plan to me, and I'll spare her," Hamas said. "There's no reason why she should be executed along with you this morning for the king's pleasure."

Deker's mind raced in circles, and to his profound amazement he found himself standing up and heard himself shouting.

"We are the Jewish people!" he cried out. "We came to this land by a miracle! God brought us back to this land! We fight to expel the non-Jews who are interfering with our conquest of this holy land!"

"So be it," Hamas said, and delivered a devastating blow to Deker's gut.

Deker collapsed to the floor, bloodied and bowed. He writhed in pain and saw flashes of light and stars and then the tip of a boot as Hamas gave him another swift kick to the face, breaking his nose.

"The last thing you will see before you leave this earth is me killing Rahab before your eyes," Hamas told him, making a gesture with his knife across Deker's neck as everything began to fade. "Then I'll make a show of killing you in front of the king. Then my ten thousand troops and I will kill Bin-Nun and all the Hebrews. As surely as the sun sets today, the world will finally be rid of your kind forever."

42

Deker kept his head up as the guards brought him outside to the vast temple court of the fortress like a condemned gladiator into the arena. At least two thousand chanting Reahn citizens were on hand to watch him burn as a sacrifice to their god Molech in hopes the deity would save them from Yahweh.

The rising sun bathed the dust on the paving stones with a golden hue in the early-morning light. The ground quaked as he walked and he could hear the Israelite war trumpets blasting in the distance. With every blast of those Israelite horns, nervous glances would erupt from the faces of the crowd for a moment before the Reahns redirected all their fear and hatred toward the prisoner. A young mother with her three children, all with the same blue eyes, watched him as he was marched past them, and began shouting.

"Molech! Molech! Molech!"

The bronze Sphinx-like visage towering above the temple court had a bull's head with two towering chimneys for horns and an immense two-story stone oven for a belly. Even now nine eunuch priests, bejeweled and dressed as horned devils, danced before Molech and fed him with sacrifices.

To his horror Deker realized those sacrifices came from a pile of several dozen human corpses beside the statue. One by one the corpses were flung into the furnace of Molech's belly, much to the delight of the crowd. Every time a corpse was consumed, Molech's eyes would turn red and smoke would erupt from his horns.

The Reahns had cleaned Deker up and clothed him in a sackcloth tunic, and painted his swollen eyelids in the way they marked their dead, but without the honor. Now they tied him to a stone obelisk in the center of the courtyard before the colossal metallic statue of their god.

The flames from Molech's belly were so high that Deker felt the heat halfway across the courtyard. But there was a method to this madness, he realized. Every time the Israelites gave a short blast of their terrible war trumpets, the priests would toss another corpse into Molech to divert the crowd.

Deker had no idea if this was the Israelites' first go-around of the morning or the seventh. At any moment a long trumpet blast would fill the air, followed by the Israelite war cry. But there would be no explosion, no "divine escalator." Instead, Bin-Nun's eight thousand troops would smash themselves to pieces against Jericho's impregnable walls while ten thousand Reahn troops picked them off until neighboring armies, seeing the carnage, would sweep in for the mop-up.

All because he, Sam Deker of the Israel Defense Forces, had brought this cataclysm upon his people and the world. Now, for the first time since Rachel died, he prayed the only prayer he knew by heart.

Hear O Israel: the LORD our God is One.

Deker lifted his eyes to see thousands of bronze helmets, gleaming spears and red, white and black banners. The faces looked like the walls surrounding him: impenetrable stone gazing down at him dispassionately on this Day of Judgment, with no sign of fear or anything else. Only the backs of the Reahn troops on the ramparts and watchtowers facing out seemed to acknowledge the eight thousand armed Israelite troops marching around the city.

Hamas knew he had already won this war before it had begun. This much was clear on his face as a gong sounded and Hamas walked out in his full military regalia before the royal tribunal seated before the pillars of the palace opposite the temple. The small, slight figure of the king sat in the center. He had the face of a bureaucrat, a caretaker, and looked lost amid all the pomp and circumstance of death.

The conductor of this symphony was clearly General Hamas, and Deker watched as Hamas with great fanfare pointed his thick finger at him for all to see.

"Behold!" Hamas cried out. "The Hebrew!"

He spoke as if that declarative statement were enough in itself to condemn Deker to death. And apparently it was.

There were no jeers now, only stone-cold silence around the outdoor courtyard. There would be no victory cheer until every Hebrew was slaughtered that day. He was simply to be the symbolic first. Just as Bin-Nun had made flint knives to circumcise his troops and unify them in heart and mind before battle, so Hamas was intent on using Deker's execution as a showpiece to rally Reah in preparation for the impending assault. And if Bin-Nun had his Phineas and Levites to contend with, Hamas had to appease Molech and his priests. To Hamas, Deker was just a piece of fore-skin to be tossed into the fires for Molech.

Another gong sounded and the elegant but weak figure of King Alakh stood up and said, "Say your last, Hebrew."

Deker said the only thing he could say under the circum-stances, which was something to support his army, his people and his faith, even if he had little to show for it.

"You hear the blast of trumpets, King Alakh!" he shouted. "You see the armies of Israel surrounding your city. You have been warned. And still you have not surrendered or spared the lives of your people by letting them leave your gates. Their blood will be on your hands, not ours. Leave now and save yourselves from total annihilation. Mark my words, this city will be rubble and dust on the ash heap of history before the sun sets today."

King Alakh looked at General Hamas and, for the benefit of the people, asked aloud, "Is what this Hebrew says true?"

"No, great King," Hamas replied.

The whole exchange seemed scripted to Deker, and he expected Hamas to produce the C-4 bricks as evidence of his suc-cess in smashing the Hebrew plot to bring down the walls.

In fact, he was hoping for it.

But Hamas produced no magic mud bricks. Instead, he dra-matically marched over to the pile of corpses by Molech and made a sweeping gesture with his hand.

"Recognize any friends, Hebrew?"

Deker stared. Four of the twisted faces on top he recognized as belonging to some of the Gadites who had joined up with Bin-Nun at Gilgal. He began to gag at the back of his throat.

The corpses being fed to Molech were Israelite troops.

"Behold the treachery of the Hebrews!" Hamas declared. "Their evil designs have been thwarted."

Panic washed over Deker as he tried to think where the soldiers had come from, what this all meant. The temple guards lifted one of the dead Gadites by the head and feet and began to swing him to and fro before flinging him into the fiery furnace for Molech to devour.

A flare from the great stone oven stabbed outward and singed the brows of one of the guards, who winced in agony but refused to cry out before Hamas, who, having firmly dug the knife of condemnation in Deker's back, decided to give it a final twist.

"This stupid, mindless spy was yet another ruse of Bin-Nun's, a decoy to the real plot to destroy us. Fortunately, they had help from one of our informants."

A side door in the fortress wall opened and out walked two Reahn guards, followed by Rahab.

43

She wore a flowing white robe with her braided hair piled on top of her head like a goddess. Deker watched her turn to face the king and tribunal. She didn't even glance at him as Hamas spoke.

"Rahab the priestess of Molech will now testify to the treachery of the Hebrews and the courage of our soldiers!" Hamas shouted out.

"The spy came to me again six nights ago," she declared. "He told me he would use magic mud bricks to open their own gate in our wall."

"Magic mud bricks," Hamas repeated for all to hear. "Are these the magic mud bricks he showed you?"

Deker craned his neck as Hamas pulled off a white cover from the stack of ten C-4 bricks on the table by the tribunal. His heart skipped a beat with hope. Somehow, should he be afforded some Samson-like moment, he would use the bricks to bring down the walls of the fortress on top of them all.

"Yes, General Hamas," Rahab replied, in a monotone that told Deker that she, too, had been carefully coached on what to say. "He told me the clay had come from the moon."

"And what did he tell you his plans were?"

"He told me the Hebrew plan was for me to harbor him six nights until today, at which point he would be given a signal to destroy our walls with these magic mud bricks. But he instead chose to disobey the orders of General Bin-Nun and attempt to bring down our walls the first night. This is when he was captured by you, General Hamas."

Hamas nodded, and then shocked Deker with his next question: "But this wasn't the real Hebrew plan, was it?"

"No," she replied.

Hamas asked, "What was the secret plan of General Bin-Nun, kept even from his unfortunate spy here?"

"The very next day, when the Israelite army first marched around our walls, six more Hebrews climbed into my window," Rahab testified. "The dust kicked up by the Israelite army circling our walls blinded our sharpshooters and provided the Hebrews the cover they required."

"And this event was repeated again each successive day until this morning, was it not?" Hamas asked her. "Every day another six Hebrew soldiers, under the cover of dust, would climb up our wall and into your cellar until all thirty-six had been assembled to carry out General Bin-Nun's true plan to bring down our city."

"Yes, General Hamas."

Deker swallowed hard. So that's why Bin-Nun had been so keen for him to secure a scarlet cord in Rahab's window, Deker realized. It wasn't to mark her house so invading troops could avoid it: it was to mark her window so these secret platoons could enter the city after him.

Hamas looked at him with hate-filled eyes and a triumphant smile. "A plan he kept secret even from this sorry spy and sacrifice before us this morning."

"Yes," Rahab said, still avoiding his gaze.

"And what exactly, Priestess Rahab, was Bin-Nun's plan for this secret force of thirty-six men?"

Rahab now turned to Deker, with anything but hate and only sorrow in her eyes. "The plan was to sneak enough troops into the city through my window to create a force just large enough to rush our guards stationed inside the main gate, kill them and then open the gate for the Israelite invaders."

Now the gasps and jeers finally erupted all around as the simplicity and audacity of the Hebrew treachery was revealed. And Deker was one of those who gasped, personally feeling the sting of betrayal not only from Rahab but more pointedly from Bin-Nun.

This was just like crossing the Jordan, Deker thought bitterly. Bin-Nun may have hoped for the best, but he had anticipated the worst. That meant he had expected Deker to fail all along with the C-4. So he instead used him to secure Plan B, which in all probability was Plan A from the get-go: sneak a covert force into the city and open the gates from the inside. Once inside, they could use battering rams to blow the walls outward. The very same plan that the ancient Greeks would use centuries later with their Trojan horse.

"And how far away is your home from the city gate?" Hamas pressed Rahab.

"It is only fifty cubits away."

Hamas nodded. "So they could rush the gate from the inside in moments and catch our men by surprise."

"Yes. As soon as they heard the signal this morning."

"And what is that signal?"

"A ram's horn, followed by a war cry."

Murmurs everywhere, and Deker didn't know if the sound was of relief that the plot had been exposed or the realization that the horn could blow at any moment and the assault would begin.

"So, at the sound of the war cry, the Israelites will rush our walls while the infiltrators rush our gate from the inside and open it to the invading Hebrew troops."

"Yes, General Hamas. That was the plan."

"*Was* the plan," Hamas said with finality as he spat at the feet of Deker. "A plan I have crushed."

Hamas let it sink in—for the king, the noblemen and military officers, and most of all for Deker, who got the distinct impression that this show was for his benefit. Not only had Hamas beaten him, but he had shown that Bin-Nun had never had any confidence in him whatsoever.

And it was all true, Deker knew. Had he just waited even a day, he would have been in Rahab's cellar to see the six new men and learn the true plan. No, he had to go ahead to save these people about to slay him as they had slain the thirty-six and soon all of Israel.

A final gong sounded and King Alakh rose to deliver the official death sentence.

"They are the Hebrews, whom their God has cursed and with whom He is so angry that He will never again be satisfied," the king said. "Israel is a warmonger to the nations, and now they are attacking us. Always they slap away the hands extended in peace and instead choose to kill everything that breathes before them."

The jeers began to grow louder now as the king continued.

"For this Hebrew spy before us, death is a judgment of mercy," the king cried out. "For he shall be a burnt offering to Molech, and his kind thereafter. May Molech feast on Hebrews for one hundred days!"

The crowd erupted into cheers as guards cut Deker from the obelisk and pointed him toward Molech with the tips of their spears. The heat from the metallic god was intense, and Deker doubted he would live to even see the inside of the furnace.

"People of Reah!" Hamas called, drawing out his sword and holding it high in the air. "With this sword I will smite the first Hebrew who falls against our walls. And with a new sword I will cut off the head of the last Hebrew alive: Joshua, son of Nun!"

The air seemed to crackle with electricity as Hamas turned to Rahab. For a wild moment Deker thought Hamas was about to throw her into the fire along with him.

"The Hebrews thought to buy your heart with gold," Hamas said to Rahab for all to hear.

"They did, General Hamas," she said, and then stepped aside to reveal her brother Ram behind her. He was carrying something in his arms. "They gave me this bowl of gold and silver coins to betray my people. I now offer these to my god Molech as a sacrifice, so you may melt them into the sword that will cut off the head of Israel forever."

Ram offered the bowl up to the sky and turned to face Deker and Molech, and Deker's throat caught at the sight of the black and red bowl—and a small unmistakable copper fuse sticking out from the coins.

44

Deker sucked in his breath and felt his heart pound in his chest as he realized that the bowl of coins was really a frag bomb that Molech was about to devour. It would detonate once the fuse lit inside the Reahn god's belly, destroying Molech and everybody else in the way of its exploding metal fragments.

The offering is a sign of her faith in Yahweh—and in me. She's really offering me a way out.

In slow motion he saw Ram hand the bowl over to Rahab, and then she in turn brought it to him. By all appearances the Reahn priestess was giving the Yahweh-worshiping Hebrew his worthless bribe to take with him to his death in the belly of the almighty Molech.

But the look in Rahab's eyes told Deker she knew very well what this bowl of coins was supposed to do, or at least what she had been told it could do before the Israelites who gave it to her were captured and killed, some or all perhaps even by her brother Ram.

Rahab stepped right up to Deker, as close as she could, to hand him the bowl. She was chanting, it seemed, but she peered intently into his eyes. The crowd began chanting and roaring along with her, and as their volume swelled she suddenly dropped her voice and spoke to him.

"Samuel Boaz Deker, listen to me: the rest of your bricks are in my cellar," she whispered in Hebrew as she handed the bowl over to him. "Elezar showed me how to push the button."

The shock had barely registered in his brain before she pulled away and he stared at her in horror. She didn't know that the C-4 exploded. She only thought it opened a wider door in a wall.

Elezar had arranged for her to blow up the lower city wall and take herself and her family out with it!

The bowl now weighed like death in Deker's hands. He simply stood there in the middle of the plaza, flat-footed, waiting for Rahab to back off with Ram, motioning with his eyes back to the gate in the far wall from which they had entered. He couldn't tell if they had made it, however, because the tip of a spear prompted him to turn his back to them and face Molech and his priests.

A drum roll began beyond view, and Deker took one inexorable step after another toward the towering monument of Molech, smoke bursting out his horns into the sky and stench-filled clouds of burnt flesh belching out his belly.

One last time he looked over his shoulder at the king and tribunal behind him with the entire palace guard. There was no sight of Rahab or Ram, although they could have remained just beyond his view.

He then felt the long spears at his back retract for a moment as the guards prepared to stab him hard and drive him headfirst into the furnace.

That was his chance.

He hurled the heavy bowl of coins in an arc into the great fire and dove to the side of the furnace, hitting the paving stones as a terrific explosion ripped open Molech's belly and blasted a million metal fragments across the temple courtyard.

45

Deker felt the blast in his ringing ears and throughout his body as he struggled to get up. The great idol of Molech, now a creaking mass of metal, collapsed into a heap with a crash. What was once a god was scattered in pieces along with the shredded limbs and charred remains of its worshipers.

There was chaos everywhere as Deker scrambled for his C-4 bricks at the heavy table next to where the tribunal had been seated. The table had been blown back on its side and shattered. The king was dead, half his face blown off. The noblemen had been cut in two through their midsections. The shrapnel had fanned out a meter above the ground, cutting down anything that had been standing.

Deker's memory flashed to what Hamas had told Rahab on her terrace the week before about the Angel of Death in Egypt. Something about natural gases rolling across the ground of Egypt to kill the firstborns as they slept. At least, that's what Deker thought he had overheard from his perch in the pergola. Today in

Jericho it was the reverse: death had felled everybody standing one meter above the ground—everybody but himself.

Deker scanned the courts. There was no sign of Hamas in the floating dust and ash. Nor of Rahab or Ram. But he found his C-4 bricks scattered behind the pieces of wood. He was able to find only eight bricks, each embedded with bits of metal, and only a single detonator still in one piece. It would have to do. He tore a bloody cape from a fallen Reahn guard, wrapped the C-4 bricks in it and threw it over his shoulder.

In spite of all the carnage around him, Deker knew he had done nothing to the wall that would advance the Israelite attack. He had to blow the north wall of the fortress.

And then somehow, someway, he had to get to Rahab's and stop her from blowing herself up before the Israelites gave their war cry.

The curtain of debris parted to reveal the iron door to the barracks in the north wall. But it also exposed him to the archers on the ramparts above, who immediately started firing down on the only moving target below.

He made a run for it in the opposite direction, toward the octagonal spire at the south wall that rose over the fortress city. The entrance door was open, the bodies of three guards and two priests on either side. He dove inside just as dozens of arrows rained down behind him.

There were shouts above and he looked up to see that a spiral stone staircase inside the tower ran all the way up to the spire. Between the voices at the top and his position at the bottom, there was a doorway to the ramparts of the fortress wall. He might have just enough time to improvise and get out of there.

He reached out and dragged in the corpse with the least damaged military uniform and helmet and threw them on. Then he quickly unpacked his C-4 and wired the bricks to his detonator inside the octagonal base of the spire. He wiped his dirty arm across his sweaty face as he worked the fuse and prayed to Yahweh it was still good. He tried to set the timer to five minutes but it displayed only two—and counting.

He swore and jumped up the stone stairwell five steps at a time and ducked out the second-story door just as three Reahns from the tower came into view.

A second later he was outside on the ramparts of the southern wall lined with hundreds of Reahn spearmen and archers. He quickly turned to his right and headed toward the corner watchtower connecting the southern wall with the western wall when the lookouts began shouting after him.

"Go see what they want!" he barked to a couple of soldiers standing in his way, and then brushed past them to the rampart tower.

Instead of following the rampart path through the tower to the western wall of the fortress, he took two flights of steps down to the lower tunnel that ran below. He pushed his way through the reserves to the end, where he climbed another stairwell to reach the rampart of the tower connecting the western and northern walls of the fortress.

As he ran along the top of the northern wall, he looked down to his left and saw the north-side slums of the city below. He could pick out Rahab's villa nestled next to the lower city wall, as well as the mass of Israelite troops out in the desert.

God, don't let them give the war cry.

Shouts rang out and Deker looked ahead to see a vengeful Hamas marching straight toward him, a bloody sword in his hand and a black cape flying off the back of his body armor. Marching behind Hamas in lockstep were hundreds of Reahn guards. The rampart shook beneath their boots.

Deker looked behind him and saw a hundred more Reahn troops emerging from the west tower, hemming him in from that direction as well.

At that moment he knew his only means of escape was to make a flying eagle leap off the wall into the city below. He began scanning the rooftops for a pile of drying flax or barley to use as a landing pad. But his eyes kept drifting down to the panicked people running through the streets as the great dust cloud of the Israelite army rolled closer and closer to the city.

Then came the explosion from inside the fortress. Hamas and all his soldiers looked up in shock as the city's great spire swayed in the sky like a giant stone palm tree, a huge gash at its base as if some divine axe had struck it.

Deker stared as the watchtower's spire blocked the sun for a second and cast a dark shadow across the rampart before it began to topple like a falling tree. He stood very still, gauging the trajectory of the fall, and didn't move.

Too late, Hamas and his Reahn guards along the middle of the northern rampart looked up to see their impending deaths. The spire crashed across the north wall, slicing clear through to the bottom before breaking into three pieces. A torrent of stones and dust billowed out from the abyss before him.

Hamas was gone, for good this time.

And then Deker heard the long blast of a horn like the trumpet of an archangel.

The Israelites were about to give their war cry.

46

Deker raced across the rooftops of the lower city toward Rahab's, jumping down into the narrow alleys between the battened-down homes as arrows started flying from the fortress archers behind him. He made it to the red-scarf district, opened the gate in front of Rahab's villa and ducked into the courtyard. The inn was deserted. He climbed down the steps to the cellar.

"Rahab!" he called out.

The door was ajar. He pushed it open and found Salmon and Achan on the floor, hands and feet lashed together, mouths gagged, eyes on fire. Rahab slipped from behind the door and rammed the tip of a sword between his shoulder blades.

"Turn around slowly or I'll kill you."

Deker slowly pivoted and saw her frightened look turn to relief as she dropped the sword and wrapped her arms around him and sobbed.

"Samuel," she sobbed. "It's all lies. I didn't betray your friends."

Deker grasped her firmly at the throat, catching her by surprise as he rammed her against the wall, next to the skulls of her own sisters.

"Then what do you call that on the floor?"

"Elezar said they were traitors."

"Elezar is dead."

"No, he's not. He left not long ago."

Deker was confused. "Where's the detonator?"

"Here." She held up her tight fist, her thumb on the button.

Slowly he lifted her thumb and then unfurled her fingers to see the detonator, and he cursed Elezar for thinking he could kill two birds—Rahab and the outer wall—with one stone.

"Untie them," he ordered, and Rahab quickly loosed Salmon and Achan, who worked his aching jaw as he rubbed his sore wrists.

Deker looked around and realized there were dozens of people huddled in the shadows of the cellar. They were all members of Rahab's family, or at least she had counted them as such. He hadn't noticed them before. The crushing gravity of the situation and lack of time pressed unbearably down upon him.

"Where are my mud bricks?" he demanded.

"In my hiding place," Rahab said.

She wiped some dirt from the earthen floor to show him a door with a thin knotted rope attached. She then lifted the door to reveal a small compartment with the explosives.

They were rigged to blow.

"Elezar," Deker cursed as he carefully deactivated the wiring and removed the bricks. "Where is he?"

"I don't know," Rahab said. "But he left you a sign. He said you would know what it means."

She pointed to the inside of the trapdoor she had propped up against the wall. Burned into it was the black outline of a dove.

The Black Dove.

Deker stumbled back on his feet, his mind reeling. As much as he hated Elezar, Deker—who questioned everything, even the legitimacy of the State of Israel itself—had never thought to question his loyalty as a Jew. And yet, the evidence was there all along that Elezar was the Black Dove, the legendary Palestinian mole within the IDF.

Suddenly it all made sense: the right-wing posturing, the image of a Jew beyond reproach, the finger-wagging at the less-than-Jews like Deker in the IDF. Most of all, it was now perfectly clear why Elezar wanted to eliminate Christianity—as well as the State of Israel before it could ever be born out of the Promised Land—by eliminating Rahab.

Worse than this revelation about Elezar was the realization that this was Deker's fault, the result of some deep, psychological defect on his part. He had been so wounded about what it meant to be a good Jew, so painfully aware of how much he fell short, that he couldn't see the hypocrisy and pretense of Elezar, who knew the Torah backwards and forwards. He was a zealot. Just not the kind of zealot that Deker had thought he was.

"What does it mean?" Salmon asked.

"Elezar has betrayed us all," Deker said as Reahn soldiers began to pound on the villa's doors outside. It would be only minutes before the Reahns stormed the cellar.

But the stab of betrayal that Deker felt didn't come from Elezar but from himself. Deker now had to question everything.

Because if he missed this, what else had he missed his entire life?

In his mind he went back to the beginning, to what Elezar could have been doing while he was testing the Temple Mount. Could Elezar have actually been the one who killed Stern? Then he went back even further in his memory, to when he had first met Elezar after the botched attempt on the Black Dove that killed Rachel.

Jesus Christ, he thought. *Elezar killed Rachel.*

47

Deker felt an ominous wind blow in through Rahab's cellar window, and a chill ran up his back as what he had been waiting for came a second later with the force of a desert storm.

The war cry of the Israelite army.

Elezar had left him with an unwinnable dilemma: blow himself up with Rahab and her family in order to open the city to the Israelites, or risk the defeat of General Bin-Nun and the Hebrews as they smashed themselves against the impregnable wall.

Rahab sensed trouble. "What's wrong, Samuel?"

Deker moved to the window and looked out at the Israelite troops rushing toward them. He then ran his fingers down the scarlet cord hanging in the window.

Bin-Nun doesn't know his thirty-six-member special-ops team is dead, Deker thought. *He thinks they're going to open the main gate from the inside.*

Another voice said, "Deker?"

This time it was Salmon talking.

Deker turned to him and said, "My plans have failed, Salmon. I did not trust Yahweh like Rahab or you or Bin-Nun. But there may yet be a way to accomplish the divine plan. You must see to it that Rahab and her family are spared."

Salmon tried to exude confidence before Rahab, but there was a cloud of doubt behind his eyes. "Where are you going?"

"To blow the main gate," Deker said as he packed the C-4 in his bag.

"You'll be slaughtered as soon as you walk out the front door," said Ram as he entered the cellar, out of breath. "We're holding them off, but you'll never get past them alive. And you'll never take out the contingent at the gate, even if we all joined you."

"I know," Deker said, and grabbed the coil of rope and moved to the window. "That's why I'm going to blow the gate from the outside."

"It's still suicide," said Ram. "If the Reahn archers don't kill you, your own advancing troops might."

"It's the only way," said Deker, suddenly calm as he gazed into Rahab's dark eyes. "It's the right way."

"There must be another way," Rahab begged him. "Yahweh has a plan."

Deker felt the throb in his throat. He never wanted to leave her. But he remained resolute. "I'm sorry, Rahab, but I believe *I* am the plan."

Rahab's eyes unlocked from his and darted over his shoulder. "Ram!"

Deker turned in time to see Ram at the window, about to climb out.

"I can no longer protect us from our own people if the Israelites fail," Ram told them. "And if the Israelites succeed, I cannot protect you from them. But these Hebrews can."

And then Ram vanished into thin air.

Deker rushed to the window and looked down to see Ram land on the ground and pull out his sword. With a shout, Rahab's big brother ran out alone against the thousands of oncoming Israelites.

"He's drawing the attention of the Reahn archers on the ramparts!" Salmon yelled, shoving his way next to Deker. "Now is our chance!"

"*My* chance," Deker told him. "You have to stay here with Rahab and keep Israel's promise."

Salmon began to protest, but Deker cut him off. "There's no time, Salmon. If you fail, her blood is on our hands, and the hands of all the kings of Israel."

Rahab rushed to him and threw her arms around him as if to keep him from leaving.

There was no time for proper good-byes, so Deker removed his IDF tag from his neck and gave it to Rahab. "This is the token of my promise to you," he said. "Your family will be safe at Gilgal tonight, and you can return it to me then." She put it on over her heart and clutched the star in her hand, as if she were willing herself to believe him.

With one last look at her, Deker sprang out the window.

48

Deker slid down the rope amid a flurry of arrows from Reahns on the ramparts above. He hit the ground unscathed and began to make his way along the base of the city wall when he heard shouting.

It was Ram, about a hundred meters out. He had fallen to his knees, his front and back shot full of arrows from both sides. He raised his sword to the sky one last time in defiance before an Israelite arrow struck him in the head and his helmet flew off before he fell back dead.

If he had any last words, Deker never heard them.

What he did hear was an unmistakable whistle, and he darted toward the gate as arrows began to rain down on him from the Reahns on the ramparts. He clung to the base of the wall as he ran toward the gate just around the corner.

Two arrows knocked him down, one in the shoulder, the other in the calf. He cried out as he landed face-first in the sand, flat on the nose that Hamas had smashed, and began to crawl meter by meter with one arm until he made it around the corner.

He managed to prop himself up against the wall, just several meters away from the gate. He looked out to see the Israelites only fifty or so meters away now.

They were coming in waves.

The infantrymen used their shields to protect the slingers, who needed both hands to counter the fire of the Reahns on the walls.

An entire line of archers, meanwhile, had dug their shields into the ground and from behind them fired at the archers in the towers. But the heavy infantry charged ahead with battering rams and close-combat spears, sickle swords and axes to smite the Reahns.

Deker pulled out his pack of C-4 and hurled the whole wired package toward the gate. It landed in the middle, just in front of the portcullis, and then he pushed the detonator.

The explosion ripped the guts of the gate out like the god Molech vomiting out his demons. A giant cloud of smoke and dust mushroomed into the air.

Ears ringing and light flashing before his eyes, Deker peered into the cloud as he snapped off the arrows in his shoulder and leg. Then the curtain parted and he saw the troops pouring through.

49

By the time Deker limped through the gate, all he could see was the flash of swords and shields. The slaughter was well under way.

The unstoppable column of Israelites snaked through the north side of the town and up through the gash in the fortress wall caused by the fall of the city's spire. People were shouting to one another but no words could be made out above the screams and shouts of battle.

From the summit, waterfalls of blood streamed down the fortress walls and into the city below, rivers of carnage floating along the streets past Deker's boots.

The dead were already piling up.

Frightened Reahns ran helter-skelter, trapped inside the walls they had erected to protect themselves. From the towers the soldiers could only watch their families die before they, too, were struck and began to fall off the ramparts as the Israelites swarmed them.

But it was the Reahn families fleeing the inescapable wrath of Yahweh, their tragic faces white with terror, that haunted Deker. The foolish among them were still trying to carry their valuables in their fine but filthy garments. The brave, mostly mothers clutching their children, wound up cornered against stone walls and run through by the merciless blades of the invading Hebrews.

The only thing escaping the city that Deker could see was its treasures: one cart after another, filled with gold ingots and silver coins and jewelry, was being wheeled out through the gate by the Levites.

Deker didn't see Phineas and suspected the priest had decided to contribute to the work of the troops in cleansing Jericho for its sins.

The Kenites, meanwhile, were lighting up bronze bowls with oil for the passing troops to dip their torches into so they could burn whatever was left of Jericho.

Deker stepped through the puddles of blood in the market square and headed toward Rahab's to make sure she was safe. Then he noticed a team of Judeans with a small battering ram heading toward a door in the city wall that he hadn't noticed before. It had a red cord hanging outside.

"Wait!" he yelled and raced to the door. "What are you doing?"

"Rahab the harlot and her family are to be spared," the commanding officer replied. He looked a bit like Salmon, and Deker guessed he might be a cousin.

"This isn't Rahab's house," Deker told them.

"But it's in the city wall."

"Her house is in the slums about fifty cubits ahead. A four-story villa overlooking a small square. You can't miss it."

"Then what's this?"

Deker stared at the red cord and shouted, "I think it's a trap!"

Sure enough, upon closer examination he saw a crude charcoal drawing on the wood.

A black dove.

"Stand guard out here," he ordered the troops. "I'm going inside. You'll block this door with carts and crates if you have to, but nobody comes out. If I don't return by the count of five hundred, see that it burns with the rest of this city to the ground."

He looked around to make sure the Judeans understood. They did, but clearly thought he was crazy and in no shape in his blood-soaked uniform to do much damage to anything as he unsheathed his sword.

"A sword may not slay this enemy," a voice said. "You may need this."

Deker turned to see old Kane step forward with his latest invention: an ancient Molotov cocktail. He held the jug with a fuse in one hand and a torch in the other.

Deker handed his sword to one of the troops and took the bomb and the torch. "A final gift to send me off, Kane? You shouldn't have."

Kane smiled proudly. Deker was actually going to miss the old warrior.

Deker didn't know why, exactly, he was so sure that he wasn't going to be walking out of the door he was about to enter. But he was sure.

"Salmon is with Rahab and her family," he told Kane with emphasis. "I've told these troops where they are. See to it that they get safely outside the city before Bin-Nun torches it."

Kane nodded. "Do your worst."

Deker opened the door, slipped inside and closed it. He immediately heard the thuds and scrapes of carts and crates stacking up behind him. Then he turned and saw the secret fail-safe to Jericho that Hamas had been hiding all along.

The shadow army.

50

Ever since Deker had heard about Jericho's shadow army, he imagined something supernatural, like demons or, more likely, some superstition. Never did he expect it to be the city's living dead.

Inside the dark tunnel, Deker immediately knew he was in the presence of thousands of bodies. The damp, rank air hung heavy with the putrid smell of rotting flesh, human waste and desperation. Now he understood why Rahab's brother Ram had refused to even speak of it. If the soldiers packed inside the upper fortress walls represented a ring of strength, then whatever rotted inside these lower city walls represented a ring of death.

Deker held up his torch to see just what exactly he was smelling. The flickering light reflected a sea of bloodshot eyes staring from pinched, pallid faces: men, women, children, even animals. This was where Hamas had crammed Jericho's sick and diseased, here inside the thick lower city walls.

What kind of defense was this? he wondered as he walked among the dying inside the city walls. These were no soldiers of Jericho.

They had no swords, no weapons of any kind, not even food. They were sick and infirm. How could they save Jericho when Hamas had condemned them to die when the walls collapsed on top of them?

Then he understood. It was all clear now.

Hamas had packed the walls with the diseased in case they did fall. Then these veritable zombies could escape to infect the Israelite troops. The troops, in turn, would infect their families. And that would be the end of the Hebrews.

This shadow army was Jericho's fail-safe that would ensure victory even in defeat. Much like Israel's fail-safe that he had sacrificed his own life to protect.

Deker covered his nose and mouth. Cholera, hepatitis B and C, jaundice, dysentery, leprosy—it was all here, and then some, plainly visible on the drawn and blemished faces. And rising above the coughs and hacks of the TB-infected was a madman laughing somewhere down the narrow corridor.

Deker could recognize that condescending laugh anywhere.

Elezar.

Deker knew that he was never going to leave these walls now, never going to see Rahab again. Not if he was to save Israel. He had to entertain Elezar long enough for the Israelites to turn the tunnels into a furnace worthy of Molech and burn them all alive before anyone could escape.

There was a doorway at the end of the section, leading to another beyond. Guarding the doorway were two ghastly-looking Reahn guards who kept the civilian sick at bay. But they didn't block him from entering the next compartment. It was as if he had been expected.

As soon as he stepped through the door, he felt a blow to his gut and doubled over as Elezar withdrew a bloody dagger from his stomach. Deker began to cough up blood.

"Welcome back, Deker," said Elezar's voice from the shadows.

Deker noticed the white salt all over the floor where his drops of blood had begun to splatter. The salt might have been stored there and cleared out, he thought, but something about it felt familiar and threw him off. He slid some of it aside with his boot and saw the flash of color. There was some kind of mosaic in the floor.

A sense of vertigo hit him and the walls seemed to bend before his eyes. As he regained his balance, he saw Elezar emerge from the shadows, laughing louder than ever.

"You did it, Deker!" he said in mock congratulation. "You finally broke."

Any other day Deker could have taken Elezar. But with the cheap stab, Elezar now had the upper hand. Overwhelmed and losing blood, Deker pulled out his Molotov incendiary.

"Your plan has failed, Elezar. Bin-Nun is going to torch the city. And I'm going to burn us all inside this furnace of death. Jericho is doomed, the future of Israel secured."

"It's Israel you have doomed, Deker, and the future of Palestine you have secured once and for all. You've just blown the Israeli fail-safe, the secret of the Tehown, the tunnel of chaos the Jews hoped to use to kill us Arabs and save themselves."

Bits of brick began to fall from the ceiling, and inside, the walls were heating up like an oven as the Israelites began to burn the city to the ground.

But Elezar beamed in triumph.

"You think you are with me in the walls of ancient Jericho

3,500 years ago, Deker. But we're not really here. We're back in a safe house in Jericho. You're strapped to a chair with a fiber-optic line sewn into your skull, and I'm pumping light waves into your brain as I interrogate you."

Deker felt the sweat coming down his face in the heat. "You're crazy! You were the one who spent days convincing me that we were in 1400 BC. You're the one who lost his mind."

"You're a fool, Deker," Elezar said. "This was all a simulation designed to break you, the bad Jew, into revealing the secret fail-safe. It has been such a simple task to guide you to this point, using your brain's own imagery to reconstruct everything about ancient Jericho along the lines of the Temple Mount to help us find the city's fail-safe and lead us to what you already knew deep inside your head."

"And what is that, Elezar?"

"Clearly, Israel's fail-safe is biological in nature. Most likely a virus created from some ancient bone fragment infected with a disease that doesn't exist in the twenty-first century. By creating a vaccine from the beginning, the Jews can release the virus and kill as many Arabs as they like and save their own people. But now that we know the threat, we can find a way to neutralize it. Now it's the Jews who will die, all because of you. Not only have you lost the Promised Land in this reality, Deker, you've lost the promised war in ours."

Deker stared at the Byzantine mosaic on the floor: it was just like the one in the holding house in Madaba—if they had ever been in Madaba. His torture could have taken place anywhere, his delusion beginning with his alleged escape from his captors.

"You're wrong, Elezar. I didn't dream this up. I never wanted to be here, so how could I be open to your suggestions?"

"All it took was the ghost of your dear Rachel in the form of Rahab to make you pant like a dog and return to your vomit."

Deker yelled and swung his torch at Elezar, who ducked. "Was that real enough for you?"

"In your mind, yes," Elezar said calmly. "In reality, no. In reality I'm about to kill you. But before I do, I thought I'd let you in on a little secret you don't know."

Deker brought his torch over Elezar's head. "It will be the last thing you say."

"Remember that little explosive you prepared for the assassination of the Black Dove? The ceremonial bowl that your beloved Rachel accidentally blew herself up with?"

"You did it," Deker accused. "I know now."

"But it wasn't me, Deker," Elezar hissed in pure hatred. "I was under orders from the IDF. The IDF was worried about your impartiality with regard to all sides of the Temple Mount. They wanted to ensure that, if push came to shove, you'd ultimately come down on the side of the Jews, and your guilt over her death was just the thing to do it."

"That's a lie!" Deker shouted.

"Is it?" Elezar said calmly. "You know it's just the sort of dirty trick the Jews have been subjecting their people to for over three thousand years."

"I've got another one here for you," Deker said, and smashed his Molotov cocktail on the floor, igniting the grains and stores around them.

As fire began to engulf them, Elezar simply looked at Deker and said, "You know what you call an Israel without Jews? Palestine!"

"We are the Jewish people!" Deker screamed, his clothing bursting into flames. "We came to this land by a miracle! God brought us back to this land! We fight to expel the non-Jews who are interfering with our conquest of this holy land!"

Just then the ground shook like a great quake. Dust came down between the bricks above, and the walls began to collapse on top of them, burying them alive. And still Elezar shouted in the dark void, his words echoing in Deker's ears.

"From the river to the sea, Deker! A Palestine without Jews!"

The curtain of dust parted, and Deker stared as an unflinching Elezar stood brazenly before him even as his clothing caught fire. His mouth widened into a macabre smile as his hair burst into flames and he was completely engulfed by the inferno.

"From the river to the sea!"

A rock from above struck Deker in the head and he collapsed into the flames. Deker felt his own life seeping from his smashed body under the relentless avalanche of stone.

Dust in his eyes, he blinked at a shaft of light through the rubble. He felt a hot wind and watched it lift the ash to reveal a flash of metal hovering over him. For a second he thought it was the face of Molech come to drag him to hell.

But it was an unmanned RQ-1 Predator drone hovering over him like a modern Angel of Death. A single Hellfire missile remained beneath its right wing. Now the remote-controlled lens of the camera in its nose cone closed in on him and then opened again.

Then the metallic Predator flew away, leaving Deker to fall into the darkness and die.

51

HADASSAH MEDICAL CENTER

Deker looked out the window from his hospital bed. The modern Abbell Synagogue in the plaza below with its famous stained-glass Chagall Windows depicting the twelve tribes of Israel told him that he was back in the present day at the Ein Kerem campus of the Hadassah Medical Center in southwest Jerusalem. Any further doubts were eliminated by the dozens of IVs, needle tracks and pangs of excruciating pain shooting up and down his battered body.

"You seem disappointed to be alive, Deker."

Deker turned to see a short, barrel-chested American in a suit standing by his bedside. It was the former U.S. secretary of defense, Marshall Packard, who more than anybody else was responsible for his transfer from the U.S. armed forces to the Israel Defense Forces several years ago. Deker now suspected the IDF had decided to return its defective merchandise to the Americans.

"The Temple Mount—" Deker said, but Packard cut him off.

"All is well," Packard assured him, then backtracked. "As well as anything concerning the Temple Mount and Jerusalem can be these days."

"And Elezar?"

"Died in the rubble by the time you were pulled out of that Palestinian house in Jericho." Packard showed Deker the display of his BlackBerry phone and played a video clip from the nose cone of the Predator drone. "The Hellfire missiles blew them back to the Stone Age."

Deker nodded. "So Elezar was the Black Dove?"

"Whatever his code name or real name might have been, Uri Elezar was definitely a PLO mole, placed inside the IDF decades ago, probably as soon as he hit puberty. Since the PLO went legit a few years back and other, more militant splinter groups began advancing the Palestinian cause through violence, we can only guess whom he really worked for when he died. We suspect it was a Jordanian cell group within an organization we call the Alignment. We could use your help fighting it when you feel better."

But Deker was still grappling with the reality that history had indeed changed. He had not made the mistake that had killed Rachel. It was Elezar who killed her. Elezar or, unthinkably, the IDF. Whatever the reality, his guilt now turned to anger. That an innocent like Rachel should suffer like that. That he should suffer still. Now the IDF was going to deny him the opportunity to confront them. They wanted him to go away, to no longer remind them of their own lapse with Elezar—or their own sin.

"When I feel better?" Deker asked. "I can barely feel anything. What did they inject me with?"

"A combination of isoniazid, rifampin, pyrazinamide, strepto-mycin and ethambutol," Packard told him. "You picked up extra-pulmonary tuberculosis in that hellhole. We had to burn it to kill anything that could breathe from getting out and spreading it."

"TB?" Deker felt around his neck for his IDF tag and knew it was missing. "No. I'm not talking about all these IVs in my arms. I want to know what those Jordanian bastards did to me."

"They weren't Jordanians, officially, but some radical Palestinian Waqf faction," Packard said. "Somehow they had gotten ahold of a new U.S. interrogation protocol that the Jordanian GID has been testing for us on rendered terrorist suspects. What they did was inject you with a genetically engineered protein from a type of pond algae that's attracted to light. This virus infected certain neurons in your brain."

Deker touched his finger to his forehead. "I felt a splinter of light."

"That's the fiber-optic cable they threaded through your skull," Packard said. "It's what enabled them to send flashes of light directly into your brain. From there they could precisely target certain neurons with light and cause them to fire. They basically took control of your nervous system."

"To probe my memories?"

"That's right. Make you talk in your sleep and extract what you knew about the fail-safe under the Temple Mount."

Deker felt empty, hollowed out, spiritless. "What's going to happen to me?"

"Fortunately, they didn't accidentally blind you, and you seem to have escaped permanent brain damage," Packard told him. "But we really don't know what the long-term effects are of infecting someone's brain with a virus that makes it susceptible to light."

Deker was quiet, thinking. "Last night I thought I woke up for a few seconds and saw my dead driver, Stern, by my bedside."

"Hmm, that's interesting," Packard said. "Like I said, we really don't know the long-term impact of your torture."

Deker asked, "So, what happens to me now?"

"You broke under torture and gave up the fail-safe. Now your superiors have come to realize that Jerusalem's only real fail-safe is the good ol' U.S.A."

"More than a few in the IDF would beg to differ," Deker said. "Israel has God on her side."

"God can't help you now, Deker. Because the IDF wants you out, one way or another. You know too much and are an embarrassment in the current political climate. So you've been dishonorably discharged to our care."

"To do what with my life?"

"That's up to you," Packard said. "When you figure it out, let me know, because we could use a man like you back home in the States."

Home.

"I have no home anymore."

"Then you'll fit right in," Packard said, and left the room.

52

THE WEST BANK

The official maps that Deker had obtained after his hospital discharge a week earlier proved worthless as he drove out in the heat from Jericho. All he had to show after three fruitless days of sifting through the sands of time were a few chips from the modern city's Oasis Casino and a hangover from too much drinking. He had already visited several other "Gilgals" around the area, tourist traps all, but none resembling the real Gilgal.

The real Gilgal.

Deker couldn't tell what was real and what wasn't anymore. Did he really take a trip through time? Or did he simply trip out on military-grade hallucinogens and live to remember it?

Still, an archaeological tour of one of those Neolithic sites along the Jordan River with a group called the Friends of the Earth had given him an idea. That site had been dug some twenty years earlier by a team from the Israel Museum and had unearthed thirteen round buildings made of mud and rock, along with agricultural facilities, including grinding stones, pounding stones, axes and sickle blades. Most interesting was a silo containing a sizable amount of wheat and barley—a fleeting image he recalled that one night in the real Gilgal.

He looked at his Landsat thematic map of the area that also included Shuttle Radar Topography Mission topographic data. It was a gift from the chief archaeology officer in the IDF's civil administration. The officer told him that this same space technology had led to the discovery of the lost city of Ubar in present-day Oman and the ancient desert frankincense trade route in southern Arabia. He only asked that if Deker actually found something, he'd let the IDF know.

The only thing Deker had found so far came from the pages of Jewish history and tradition. From multiple sources he was able to piece together a general picture of what happened to Rahab and the rest he had met back in time or in his mind. He played the scenario over and over like a movie while he searched for Gilgal.

Rahab and her family were indeed spared death and allowed to live outside the Israelite camp at Gilgal. She almost immediately married Salmon, the son of Nahshon. Rahab shortly thereafter gave birth to a son they named Boaz. Deker wasn't quite sure what to make of that, and for the time being buried it in his heart. When Boaz had grown, he married a woman named Ruth and they had a son, Obed, who had a son named Jesse, who had a son named David.

David became the king of Israel, fulfilling the prophecy of the six-pointed conjunction of stars in the heavens that Rahab had pointed out to Deker that night on her terrace so long ago. Fourteen generations later, from the line of David, came Jesus, whom his Roman executioners called the "King of the Jews" and whose cousin John the Baptist called the "Passover Lamb" who would take away the sins of the world.

Tracing Rahab's bloodline to Christ made Deker think back to the scarlet cord in Rahab's window, and to her faith that Yahweh would "pass over" her sins as the Angel of Death had passed over the Hebrew slaves in Egypt. Her faith had been rewarded, and so had Salmon's.

But would his? Deker wondered.

Salmon's curious friend Achan bin-Zerah wasn't as fortunate. He apparently had defied General Bin-Nun's *herem*, or ban, on keeping any spoils from Jericho by pocketing two hundred shekels of gold and silver during the pillage instead of turning them over to the Treasury of Yahweh. Bin-Nun figured this out days later when he sent a small unit of thirty-six troops drawn from a single division to capture the town of Ai. A small and easy target compared to Jericho, to be sure, but the Israelites were ambushed and killed. After another face-to-face meeting with Yahweh, Bin-Nun used a mass form of divination—casting lots—to identify Achan as the cause, and had him stoned to death along with his wife, children, sheep and every breathing thing he owned. Then Bin-Nun had them burned and buried under the pile of rocks used to kill them.

From then on, Joshua, the son of Nun, moved from one victory to another in his quest to claim the Promised Land for Israel from the Jordan River to the Mediterranean Sea. He split Canaan in two, first taking out the southern kingdoms before turning his attention to the more powerful northern kingdoms. He even gave Phineas a sign to remember forever when, according to the book of Joshua, the sun stood still for an extra day so the Israelites could kill more enemies in a decisive victory. Only Jerusalem remained untaken.

Deker knew that Bin-Nun's plan to cut the land of Canaan in half was the very strategy that modern Israel's Arab enemies had long harbored for wiping the Jewish state off the map. To avoid such a fate while he was in charge, Bin-Nun focused on defending Israel's moral boundaries even more than her natural ones. He was especially concerned about the threat of other religions in Canaan, which ultimately came to roost with King Solomon, who for all his wisdom allowed the influence of his many foreign wives to persuade him to turn the six-pointed Star of David into the official emblem of the state.

"But as for me and my family," Joshua bin-Nun proudly declared, "we will serve the Lord."

Finally, before he died, Bin-Nun signed a treaty in which Israel pledged to honor other nationalities in Canaan who honored Yahweh. He signed it at Shechem, the place where God first promised Abraham the land of Canaan.

Surely this must have pleased Rahab.

Reading through these historical documents, Deker had even begun to at least understand the rationale behind Bin-Nun's strategy of incinerating entire cities and every man, woman, child and animal that breathed inside their walls. Due to the tuberculosis the doctors had discovered in his lungs at Hadassah Medical Center, Deker did some research and learned that archaeologists had also discovered history's earliest evidence of TB in ancient bones buried under Jericho. Such airborne diseases were rampant in ancient times. Israel, therefore, faced an existential threat any time she came into contact with her enemies. Incineration was the only insurance to counter the threat in that age.

So at least Bin-Nun had had his reasons. And so, perhaps, did Israel today.

All the same, Deker knew he would never be able to erase from his mind that first horrific glimpse of twenty-four thousand blackened corpses strung out among a golden sea of shittah trees.

53

GILGAL

The sun beat down ever hotter as Deker approached the site of his latest candidate for Gilgal. This one had a familiar grade with a few ancient redbud trees bent in a way Deker had seen only once before. Deker was still consumed by an obsession for the truth that his discharge from the IDF and the offer to rejoin the Americans had only inflamed.

He took a shovel and started digging, continuing long after the sun went down and the moon came up.

Then he struck something.

He shined a light on the slab of rock and felt his heart jump when he saw the seal engraved on the surface: the sign of Judah.

It was one of the dolmen stones, but considerably smaller—maybe half of its original size, as though it had been cut or broken in two.

He felt a surge of hope and spent the next two hours digging around the slab, ultimately using his Jeep's winch to pull it out and reveal the silo beneath it.

The silo was still filled with grain so old and cracked, it was like dust. Simply inhaling made him breathe it in and he coughed. He tied a cloth around his mouth like a surgical mask and dug through it until he struck something else.

It was a small bronze box with a crescent moon on it.

Just like Rahab's jewelry box.

His heart skipped a beat.

He blew away the dust and cracked open the box.

As soon as he saw what was inside, he fell to his knees, weeping for no reason he could name. A moment later, after he had composed himself, he removed it.

His IDF tag with the Star of David.

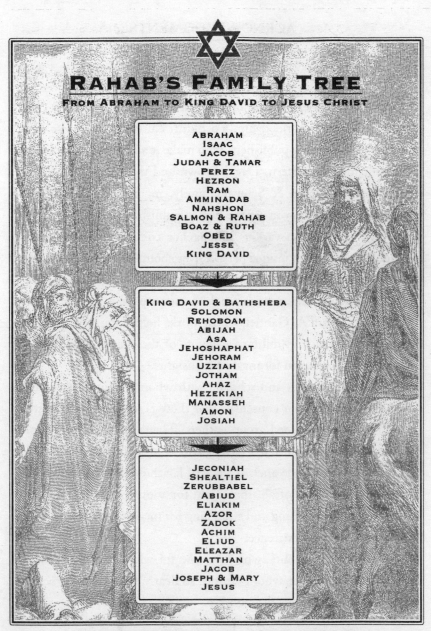

RAHAB'S FAMILY TREE
FROM ABRAHAM TO KING DAVID TO JESUS CHRIST

ABRAHAM
ISAAC
JACOB
JUDAH & TAMAR
PEREZ
HEZRON
RAM
AMMINADAB
NAHSHON
SALMON & RAHAB
BOAZ & RUTH
OBED
JESSE
KING DAVID

KING DAVID & BATHSHEBA
SOLOMON
REHOBOAM
ABIJAH
ASA
JEHOSHAPHAT
JEHORAM
UZZIAH
JOTHAM
AHAZ
HEZEKIAH
MANASSEH
AMON
JOSIAH

JECONIAH
SHEALTIEL
ZERUBBABEL
ABIUD
ELIAKIM
AZOR
ZADOK
ACHIM
ELIUD
ELEAZAR
MATTHAN
JACOB
JOSEPH & MARY
JESUS

(SOURCES: THE BOOK OF RUTH AND THE GOSPEL OF MATTHEW)

ACKNOWLEDGMENTS

To Emily Bestler and Simon Lipskar, my editor and agent, for your support and friendship. To Judith Curr, Louise Burke and Carolyn Reidy, my publishers, who make it all possible. To Sarah Branham, Laura Stern, David Brown and the rest of the Atria, Pocket and Simon & Schuster family, my deepest thanks and respect to you all—you are the best in publishing.

To members in various intelligence communities who provided me with their unique perspectives about the three-thousand-year-old struggle that forms the backdrop to *The Promised War,* your humanity impresses as much as your expertise. To historians such as Richard A. Gabriel, whose works helped me reconcile the ancient biblical and military accounts of the events described in my novel, thank you for invaluable insights.

To those rabbis and scholars with whom I consulted, thank you for sharing your consensus that there is no consensus whenever such an esteemed group gathers. Thank you in advance for overlooking the inevitable errors and contradictions of my fictional account of the ancient siege of Jericho—they are mine and mine alone. Most of all, thank you for showing the humility of students still searching and stretching for meaning in a world that seems to deny its existence.

To my wife, Laura, who loves me for who I am, and to our boys, Alex and Jake, whom we love so dearly, thank you for being the joy in my journey through life.